Secrets, Lies, and Pies

Lisa Hall

9/30/07

Akemi,

Happy reading! Hope you enjoy your first trip to Coleman. Come back for the sequel!

Lisa Hall

Mountain Girl Press
Bristol, Virginia

Secrets, Lies, and Pies

Mountain Girl Press
Established 2005

Cover art by Pam Keaton

You may contact the publisher at:
Mountain Girl Press
P.O. Box 17013
Bristol, VA 24209-7013
E-mail: publisher@mountaingirlpress.com

ISBN: 978-0-9767793-2-2

To all the ladies who have ever kept a secret, confronted a lie, or baked a pie

Chapter 1

"Oh gee, here he comes!"

Every Friday afternoon, Marlene was graced by the presence of Glen Davis. The encounters had been going on for more than twenty years with a short and welcomed reprieve for the six months that Glen was engaged to Tammy Rhiner. Marlene wondered if his visits would continue for the rest of their natural lives. Would this guy ever get the hint?

Funny, there was a time when the very presence of Glen Davis made Marlene, and most other girls for that matter, giddy. He definitely peaked in high school. Those were his glory days. He was a defensive lineman on the football team, point guard on the basketball team, and first baseman for the baseball team. He walked the halls side-by-side with his jock buddies and a slew of lovesick girls trailing behind him. On the weekends, he threw legendary parties in his parents' basement. That is, until he got caught having one of his wild shindigs. Then the decline of Glen Davis began. It wasn't a slow decline. It was sharp and sudden, like a downhill crash.

Glen's parents came home early and unexpectedly one night to find he and half the high school engaged in all sorts of underage debauchery in their basement. Glen's mom told people, "We heard strange noises downstairs. When his father and

I got to the bottom of the steps, it's like we walked onto Bourbon Street in New Orleans."

That marked the end of his raging keg parties and the beginning of his tumble down the high school hierarchy. Glen later failed three of his classes, making him ineligible to play sports. Pretty soon, Glen was just an average Joe instead of Joe Athlete, trying to get a date and acting like he was still cool.

Marlene felt bad for him and agreed to be his date to the Senior Prom. Glen repaid her by spreading rumors that they had gone back to his house and committed more sin in his parents's basement than had occurred in all the combined parties he'd ever had. In all actuality, they did go back to his parents' house. They watched a movie. Glen fell sound asleep, and Marlene quietly excused herself and walked the two blocks from Glen's house to hers.

Unfortunately, Glen's claims were backed up by Charlotte Holt. Charlotte lived across the street from Glen. Charlotte's parents had forbidden her to attend the prom because they did not approve of the type of dancing that went on. Sadly, Charlotte sat in front of their living room's bay window all night and watched as Glen and other kids in her neighborhood emerged in pastel tuxes, ruffled dresses with hoop skirts, and wrist corsages on stretchy silver elastic.

Charlotte retired to her bed around eleven thirty, but was awakened when Glen's car pulled back into the driveway. Charlotte grew very curious about what might be going on at Glen and Marlene's little post-prom celebration. Glen and Charlotte had known each other since they were four, and Charlotte hoped with all her heart that Glen would one day notice her as more than just the girl across the street.

Charlotte couldn't keep herself from getting up when she heard Glen's car. She sat glued in her parents beige wing-back chair in front of that living room window. For hours, Charlotte sat quiet and still in the dark, like a private detective on a stake-out.

Charlotte grew despondent as the clock struck 2:00 am and Glen still had not fired up his Mustang to take Marlene back to her house. She seethed as she imagined the hot exchanges of passion. Yes, she feared that the basement across the street was becoming a den of iniquity. All of Charlotte's fantasies about Glen coming to realize that he had secretly loved her all along and saving himself for their wedding night came to a crashing halt.

Suddenly, around 3:00 am, Charlotte caught a glimpse of dark satin. Marlene had dared to break from the standard Easter egg hued tulle and had chosen a more mature, fitted, deep burgundy gown with a slit that ended a little beyond her knee. Most thought Marlene's choice showed sophistication. Charlotte allowed that it looked provocative and inappropriate.

When Charlotte saw Marlene walking home at that time of the morning, holding her shoes in one hand, hiking up that dress in the other, she felt she knew exactly what had happened. Her momma had always told her that guys would quickly be done with a girl who did not protect her virtue. "They're just like trash. They get used, then discarded," is what her momma told her.

Glen had gotten his way with Marlene, and then had thrown her to the curb. Charlotte just knew in her gut that it or some similar scenario had occurred. Better yet, what if Marlene had been too forward, and Glen made her leave before anything at all happened?

Charlotte hoped that the lack of respect shown for Marlene meant that Glen was ready for a girl like her. The next day, right after she'd had a big Sunday lunch at her Grandmother's house; Charlotte marched over to Glen's front door in her favorite ruffled Sunday frock. The hem stopped just above her knee, and she had forgone hosiery. It was a flash of skin that her grandmother had noted her disapproval of at the family's Sunday lunch. This was a flirtin' outfit, and rules had to be broken!

She laid out all of her feelings for him and hopes for their future. With all the cards on the table and her pride long gone,

Charlotte waited for Glen to sweep her off her feet and give her a big romantic kiss, just like in the movies. Instead, Glen just stood there silent and uncomfortable for a couple of minutes and then let Charlotte know that even though he was flattered, she was not his type. Glen handled it better than most would ever give him credit for: but Charlotte took it hard, just the same. She cried all afternoon and into the night. Her eyes were so swollen on Monday morning that she skipped school.

By the time Charlotte came back to school on Tuesday, Glen's self-perpetuated rumor about him having his way with Marlene on prom night had made its way through the school. Charlotte was hurt and angry and out for revenge! She embellished Glen's story by describing Marlene's lonely early morning walk home in her prom dress. "Marlene's walk of shame" is how Charlotte depicted it.

Marlene confronted them both in a less than calm way. Glen has groveled for her forgiveness and another chance ever since. Charlotte, on the other hand, realized that there was a certain power and intrigue that came with being the gossip queen of the school. Suddenly, people wanted to be around her. They were only interested in hearing the nasty things she had to say about others, but Charlotte did receive some long desired attention nonetheless.

Glen, thanks to his dad, was able to secure a good job in his family's fencing business. The area was full of farms, meaning there were miles and miles of fencing to secure all the livestock. He never failed to mention to Marlene that he made good money and had the toys to show for it. "We'll have to go riding around in my Corvette on some pretty day. I'm headed out to the lake this afternoon. Gonna take a ride in my Mastercraft speedboat. You'll have to hang out at my house sometime and watch a movie on my brand new big screen with surround sound."

Everything he had was "state of the art, fully loaded, best you can buy, special edition, custom, or top of the line." If Glen himself were rolled in gold and sprinkled with diamonds, he still would not have appealed to Marlene.

If Glen ever forgot to exercise bragging rights, his momma took the liberty.

She came into Marlene's store, Cutie Pies, quite often, mentioning to Marlene how well Glen was doing. "Glen hates to brag. You'd never hear this from him, but he just secured a huge fencing contract with one of the biggest dairy farms in the region. Have you seen Glen's house? It's four thousand square feet, sits on three acres, and has a Jacuzzi and in-ground heated swimming pool."

Hates to brag! Maybe he learned from his momma!

After high school, while most sought employment or higher education, Charlotte was initiated into the ranks of the most underhanded, devious, and destructive group of women in town. Charlotte immersed herself into their scheming and slander. With her help, they took it to a new level, becoming more calculating and organized. They became gossips on a mission. They were malicious with intent. They hoped to rule the town by destroying the reputation of each and every person that had ever crossed them or made them feel inferior in any way. They called themselves "The Coleman Canasta Club." The whole town knew playing canasta was just a cover in that it provided a legitimate excuse for them to meet on a monthly basis. If there were a regulating commission for canasta, someone would have reported these women. They tarnished what was supposed to be a wholesome gathering of women engaged in light-hearted competition and made it into grudge match. They didn't even know how to play the game! Why, Jen Lunsford told everyone that she didn't believe in playing cards or anything that could be even loosely linked to gambling. How ironic that she was in the Canasta Club! They probably didn't even have a deck of cards present at their monthly events. No, Canasta Club was just a front; a bit like the mafia, except they laundered rumors.

Everyone in town who was not in the Canasta Club called them The Hens!

How did people come up with that name? Canasta Club members always had an affinity for their knickknacks. Most had small collections that could be contained on what-not shelves, window sills, and curios cabinets. Some took collecting more seriously; filling their homes and yards with thousands of objects. One or two even had to add an extra room to their homes or rent storage units.

One that really took collecting to the extreme was the founding member of The Canasta Club, the head honcho, the grand dame, the patron saint, the mother of all Hens. Mary Thornton, who is now deceased, was the one who formed The Canasta Club. Mary was a nice lady, with a generous heart, and a wonderful sense of humor. She truly did form the organization as a way for ladies to get together, celebrate friendship, and enhance their sense of community. They used to do lots of charity work; collecting toys and coats for disadvantaged children, heading up food drives, bake sales, and auctions. It was a good and decent organization that did things to benefit the disadvantaged. After Mary's passing, The Coleman Canasta Club became something else entirely, and Mary would be so disappointed.

Mary had a huge collection of hens. It began when she remodeled her kitchen in a hen and egg theme. Then, everybody began buying Mary hens for holidays. Before long, Mary even had a tag on the front of her car that said "Hen Lady." She wore a golden hen pin on her lapel, used stationery with hens on it, and her checks had hens on them, too. Mary's daily life was infused with hen stuff. The name began being used for the whole club. The name used to pay homage to their founder. It stuck because it aptly described a group of women who sat around and clucked and pecked away at the reputations of their neighbors.

Chapter 2

Food trends, they're ever-changing as the seasons. A few years ago, serving fancy cupcakes at weddings was all the rage. Next, brides and grooms across the country invested in colossal towers of carefully stacked sticky glazed donuts. It was predicted by some, in the know, that pies would become the next big thing. Yes, pretty soon, tables at reception halls across the nation would be brimming over with pies.

How long would it take for this trend to make its way to the tiny hamlet of Coleman, Virginia? It would take some time to trickle down from New York, creep up from Atlanta, or shimmy east from California. You'd better believe, when it did, Marlene Prescott would be ready!

Marlene was Coleman's premier baker and perhaps the most successful business woman in town. This, along with her beauty and cool demeanor stirred up big batches of jealousy among The Hens mostly because these ladies had squandered their lives finding fault with others instead of creating good things for themselves. It couldn't help but be noticed that most of them had also let themselves go in the looks department.

At forty-one Marlene was lovelier than ever. She kept her auburn hair in a short messy style that flipped in the back and was streaked throughout with butterscotch highlights. Marlene's complexion was perfect, glowing, and medium in tone. The only clues to her age were the slight crinkles that formed around her enormous green eyes when she smiled. A light and random sprinkling of freckles gave her a fresh, fun, youthful look.

Marlene was five foot six and most of that was leg! Thanks to genetics and working out whenever time allowed, she had a figure that most twenty year olds would envy. While Marlene had too much class to dress in provocative clothing, she didn't exactly downplay her assets either. Marlene walked that fine line of wearing things that flattered and turned heads without looking trashy. While most women in Coleman thought Marlene looked fantastic, and tried to emulate her style, that certain little group thought all women over the age of thirty ought to be covered from head to toe in denim jumpers or patterned muumuus.

Marlene was well aware of the fact that she was being discussed. It was mostly good for a laugh. Sometimes she and her friends joked that one of them should infiltrate "The Hens," disguised in a big ill-fitting garment, disastrous hair, and nasty attitudes. They would have done something to get back at The Hens if they weren't too busy having a life. Besides, they knew that eventually these ladies would get caught in their own snare, bramble, chicken poop, or whatever it was that fine feathered farm creatures got caught in!

Chapter 3

When Marlene was a little girl, she spent nearly every weekend at her grandparents' farm. On Saturday mornings, Marlene and her grandmother would get up in the wee hours of the morning to make fried pies. They'd roll out dozens of little circles of pie crust dough, slather it with various sweet fillings, fold the circles over to enclose the fillings, and then drop the pies into hot shortening. They'd work for a couple of hours until they had several dozen and about four or five varieties. Apple, blueberry, and peach were the most popular flavors. Whenever possible, they used fruits and berries her grandfather grew himself. After they came out of the fryer, the pies got a generous shake of cinnamon and sugar.

Marlene's grandmother had found out the hard way that fried things got soggy if they were closed up tight. After too many batches of her picnic chicken had lost the crunch from the crust, she began experimenting with various modes of transporting fried treats. Finally, she discovered that plain brown paper sacks kept the food warm, but allowed it to breathe just enough to keep it crisp and fresh. In her neatest handwriting, Marlene would label each bag with the type of pie it contained and the two ladies would take their warm pies to the county stockyard.

Farmers hauled their cattle to sell at the stockyard on Saturday mornings. Hungry farmers would get one whiff of those little twenty-five cent pies and be lined up thirty or forty deep. Before long, the duo was making a profit. Marlene's grandma invested in a giant coffee urn and a bulk load of disposable cups. They sold coffee for a nickel a cup to wash down those pies.

When Marlene's grandfather passed away, her grandma stepped up production in order to support herself. The two gals had to come up with a name that was catchy. They honored the memory of Marlene's grandfather who always called her "cutie pie." Soon, Cutie Pies became a Coleman icon. There were so many people coming to the stockyard just to visit their pie booth that the stockyard parking lot was filling up with cars. This didn't sit well with the farmers because they didn't have room to park their cattle trailers. The owner of the stockyard had to hang up signs asking that non-agricultural vehicles park in the lot across the street.

With the life insurance money from her grandfather, Marlene's grandma purchased a historic building in downtown Coleman. Of course, fried pies were still the cornerstone of the business; but she also expanded into tarts, cream pies, fruit pies, you name it. Ever loyal to those who got her started; Marlene's grandma purchased a food service trailer so that every Saturday morning Marlene could continue to sell pies and coffee to the farmers at the stockyard.

When Marlene's grandmother died, eight years ago, Marlene inherited the business. Always the big dreamer, Marlene expanded on what she and her grandmother had begun in that little farmhouse kitchen. Cutie Pies became one of the most successful businesses in town. Marlene's pies were so legendary that tourists would exit the interstate and go thirty minutes out of their way just to buy a pie. She and her pies were written about in regional and national magazines and travel guides. Amazingly, Marlene did everything herself. The pies were baked, sold, and delivered by Marlene.

As much as The Hens wanted to speculate about how Marlene spent her evenings and why she wasn't married, the truth was plain and simple. Marlene was all-consumed with making pies.

She could have had a more exciting social life. After all, she had this sexy Betty Crocker thing going on, which attracted men like crazy! Instead of running around, she was running a business. Morning, noon, and night, she baked, developed recipes, and did business related paperwork. "Let The Hens say all they want!" was Marlene's attitude. She was having a ball and making a pretty penny in the process. Marlene wasn't the least bit worried about getting even. Success was the best revenge.

Chapter 4

Marlene had a morning appointment with her accountant, Larry McCrumb. If Larry weren't the only CPA in town he probably wouldn't have had any clients. Larry was never the problem. He was a fine accountant, professional, meticulous, and honest as the day was long. The problem was Patsy, his nosy wife. Patsy operated under the guise of being her husband's secretary, but all she really did was snoop around to find out how much money people made and who was being audited. Worse yet, she reported her findings to The Hens.

Because Patsy really had no productive function at the office, Larry had Dorothy working as his "assistant." That really meant that Dorothy did the work that his "secretary" should have been doing. The only reason Larry allowed Patsy to "work" for him at all is that she would have spent him into bankruptcy if she were home all day. He paid her a small salary, which was a pittance compared to what she could spend if she were turned loose every day with his credit cards, home shopping channels, and too much time on her hands.

Dorothy's maiden name was Pittman, so in school, she and Marlene were thrown together in the scheme of all things alphabetical. They quickly became little partners in crime. It didn't take long for them to officially get in trouble together.

On their first day of kindergarten, Marlene and Dorothy got sent to the principal's office. It was a beautiful day, too pretty to be stuck inside. Marlene and Dorothy decided it would be a lovely day for a picnic. While their teacher was helping Timmy Miller open his milk carton, the girls grabbed their trays and snuck out of the cafeteria. They made their way to the playground and hunkered down on the merry-go-round to finish lunch al fresco style. The impromptu picnic soon came to an abrupt ending. Katie Beck saw them sneak out. There was never any love between Katie and Marlene. Katie's momma, Ella, used to date Marlene's dad. She claimed Marlene's momma stole him from her. For years, Ella told anyone who'd listen how Marlene's momma was sneaking and underhanded and had ruined her life. She did this long after she'd married Katie's daddy, which must have made him feel like a second place ribbon. Katie had a mouth on her like her momma.

That prissy little tattle tale told on Marlene and Dorothy. She started yelling, "Marlene, you're a sneaky little rotten rat just like your mother!"

Mr. Owen, the principal, organized a full-scale manhunt. Within five minutes they were found and punished. The girls tried to plead ignorance of the school rules; after all, they were only in kindergarten; but Mr. Owen wouldn't buy it. He launched an attack on their backsides that they would forever remember. That set in motion years of mischief and torments the two unleashed upon the community!

When Marlene and Dorothy were in the second grade, Katie Beck's daddy got a promotion that sent them out of town. Allison Zimmerman moved to Coleman when her dad got Mr. Beck's old job. For Marlene and Dorothy, switching out Katie for Allison was a good trade. Marlene and Dorothy knew they had to make their dastardly duo into a trio. The three saw more fun and misdeeds growing up than a dozen mean little boys.

The three of them couldn't have been more different in some ways. Marlene was always the foxy, curvy, sophisticated one, who was also extremely creative, artistic and gutsy. Allison was the pretty blond cheerleader with lots of spunk and a sassy attitude. Dorothy, she was the most organized and practical of the three. Dorothy was also the shortest of the three, standing five foot one in sock feet. She tended to be about ten pounds overweight unless dieting or on a fitness kick.

The bane of her existence was an unruly mop of brown hair. It was thick, coarse, and very curly. There were a few days a year when the humidity was around zero and Dorothy's hair looked really good. On those days, she wore it down in loose curls and people said, "Oh your hair is so beautiful! I'd kill to have curls like that. Why don't you wear it down more often?"

On most days, she piled it into a ponytail or made a French braid. Many people complimented her big blue eyes, but otherwise, she thought of her face as pretty average. There was nothing bad about it, but nothing besides her eyes that Dorothy thought stood out. Dorothy described herself as more pleasant looking than pretty.

Marlene was the dreamer, and Allison tended to be a little spastic and impulsive. Dorothy was the one who kept a cool head. When they were in school, the three were often put in charge of organizing various school events. Dorothy would raise the money and delegate responsibilities. Marlene would come up with a theme, décor, and food. Allison would be in charge of getting the word out.

Whenever Dorothy sensed they were headed for more trouble than they could get out of, she was the one who kept it from going too far. "Slow down; let's stop and think about this; are you sure you really oughta?" are all things Dorothy said frequently when they were growing up.

Still, she was no kill-joy; plenty enough meanness went on. Dorothy only stopped the fun when there was risk of being arrested, seriously injured, or killed. All-in-all, the girls had more than their fair share of fun!

14

While Marlene ran Cutie Pies, and Dorothy worked for Larry, Allison was a stay-at-home mom. For several years, she worked as a nurse and was quite good at it. She was employed at the hospital in Langrid, where she advanced to a supervisor's position. At first, she and Gary didn't think they would have kids. They both loved their careers and enjoyed having the freedom to travel. Suddenly, her biological clock kicked in and threw Allison into a 180-degree turn. She got pregnant, quit her job and was never happier. She prayed that neither of her kids would wind up being as mean she and her two best friends were! Allison, Dorothy and Marlene all changed, but remained close. They had to watch themselves. Sometimes those mean streaks still wanted to rear their ugly heads!

Marlene and Dorothy chatted for a minute while Marlene waited to see Larry. The coffee maker was close to Dorothy's desk. Patsy, his wife, had just made a fresh pot ten minutes before; but she came over, dumped it in the sink and made a new pot. As she fumbled for the coffee filters, she leaned in their direction. Making coffee was Patsy's preferred method of snooping. She made about ten or twelve pots a day! She drank at least one cup from every pot to make sure it wasn't too strong. Not only did her breath reek of coffee, coffee smell wafted out of her every pore. Coffee and cheap perfume, that's how one knew that Patsy McCrumb had entered a room.

Patsy complained often of nervous twitches and insomnia and couldn't understand what was causing her afflictions. Here's a clue! Perhaps it was the dozen or so cups of java she took in every day. Dorothy suggested once that she could try cutting back on caffeine to see if that would help her jitters and sleep problems. Patsy quickly dismissed the suggestion saying "No, I know that's not what's causing it!"

Once, Larry had Dorothy secretly switch all the coffee to decaf. Patsy could tell her coffee had been tampered with on her first sip.

When Larry came out to tell Marlene he was ready to see her, Patsy followed them into his office asking if they wanted coffee. They declined Patsy's offer and she reluctantly stepped out. Marlene was seeing Larry because she had finally decided to spend a little less time at the shop. She had found a young lady who was taking culinary arts courses at the local technical institute. The girl had come highly recommended from all of the instructors. Marlene hoped she'd found someone she could trust to run Cutie Pies when she wanted to take some time off. Marlene was meeting with Larry to find out how to set her new employee up with benefits. If this girl was as good as Marlene hoped, she wanted to hang onto her!

There was another more personal financial matter that had Marlene seeking Larry's advice. After much discussion and a few tears, Marlene and her parents had been thinking about selling her grandparents' farm.

Marlene's parents moved to Florida a few years ago. They hung onto the farm just in case they didn't like Florida. Marlene's dad thought, at first, that they might wind up coming back to Coleman and building a house on the land. They had grown to love Florida so much that they planned to stay there until the Lord called them home.

Until recently, they wanted to lease the farm. Just last month, an unexpected call changed their plan. Last year, plans were announced to build an interstate that would include an exit ramp leading to Coleman. Since the announcement, several businesses expressed interest in relocating to Coleman. A manufacturer got in touch with Marlene's father, offering to purchase the entire farm. The company offered more money than they could ever get from leasing the land to someone. They hated to think about letting it go, but it seemed best for the whole family. Besides, Marlene's grandparents would never have wanted the farm to become a burden on the family.

When they looked at the big picture, it seemed to be for the greater good. The company's process did not pollute the environment and the jobs were needed. It would be good for their family as well as the community.

Larry wasn't technically a financial advisor, but he'd seen good and bad investments that various people in Coleman had made. Most importantly, he was a trusted friend; and Marlene felt his advice would be sound.

Marlene would receive a portion of the money from the sale. She was torn between buying the building next to Cutie Pies or putting the money into a retirement account. The building next door had gone up for sale. It would be easy enough to knock out a wall and make it into one big space. Although purchasing the building next door would be the more risky of the two choices, Marlene got excited when she contemplated the possibilities of expanding her business.

After explaining her dilemma to Larry, he carefully considered what she had told him and then replied "Oh, you need to invest that money in some retirement accounts."

Marlene's heart sank a little. "Yeah, I guess you're right. I'm too old to go throwing money around at something that may not work out."

A big smile came across Larry's face. "Marlene, I'm just messing with you. Buy that building next door! It's what you really want to do. Besides, owning real estate is like money in the bank. Buy that place today, before somebody else realizes that commercial property in Coleman will double in price after that interstate ramp is built. You're a smart business lady. You'll make it a success!"

Patsy was on the phone with Ingrid Miller. Naturally, they were discussing Marlene. Patsy allowed that Marlene had put on a couple of pounds and that her latest hair color came out a little too red. For the life of her, she couldn't figure out why Marlene was there when it was nowhere close to tax season. The combined sharp wits of Ingrid and Patsy eventually surmised that Marlene must have been having financial problems.

"In over her head" are the words Patsy uttered. Patsy whispered to Ingrid "I know she makes good money with that business, but there are a lot of expenses. I bet she doesn't have any idea how to properly manage her money. She's never seemed too smart if you ask me."

Nobody ever asked Patsy anything! She gave her opinion regardless and The Hens took it as the gospel, as if everything that came out of Patsy's mouth had been inspired by God himself.

Well, God certainly would not use Patsy McCrumb as his messenger. In fact, he must have been quite displeased with her for being so malicious. She may feel a great wave of conviction someday! Dorothy had half a mind to walk right over to Patsy's desk and set her straight, but why bother? Patsy and all her silly friends would believe what they wanted. Dorothy took satisfaction in traveling on the high road. Besides, she began to think it might be fun to watch The Hens get a little egg on their faces!

Chapter 5

There were two places in Coleman for ladies to get their hair done. The pin-curled and teased went to Leila's. The rest went to Curly-Q's. There were few exceptions to this rule. The women of the Patton family did not cut their hair for religious reasons. Bridgett Moreland visited her mom in Atlanta every six weeks and had her hair done down there at a fancy salon. Bridgett claimed that her stylist used to cut Jane Fonda's hair when Jane was married to Ted Turner. She said they even let customers have champagne while their color processed. Reba Coffey wore a bowl cut all her life. She went to the Coleman Barber College and had her cut maintained for five bucks a pop, tip included. Everyone else goes went to either Curly-Q's or Leila's.

Curly-Q's patrons arrived for their appointments clutching pictures of their favorite celebrities to show their stylist. Everyone showed up at Leila's empty-handed and asked for "the usual." The interior of Curly-Q's was done in earth tones with some animal print accents. Soothing instrumental music played softly from a state-of-the-art sound system. The waiting area was furnished in comfy overstuffed chairs and black lacquered tables stacked with fashion magazines. Leila's had a concrete floor that was painted burnt orange. The walls were covered in olive green and brown wallpaper. The waiting area held two metal folding chairs with a big wooden spool between them. In the middle of the spool was a glass bowl with Hall's Cough Drops and a box of tissue. The countertops at the stylists' stations were harvest gold with flecks of metallic. It was total seventies, but not kitschy or retro, just outdated and garish.

The hairdos created in Leila's lagged a couple of decades behind the seventies décor. The coifs were more nineteen fifties, requiring the ladies to sit under hooded dryers and then have their hair teased to the sky. The customers were not particularly nostalgic. They just didn't seem to realize that styles changed. Just as Leila's customers seemed oblivious to the passing of decades, they also seemed to take no interest in the actual time of day. No clock was needed in Leila's salon. The passing of one soap opera into another marked time on an old television mounted in the corner. The reception was lousy, but Leila had become an expert at adjusting the rabbit ears, beating the side of the television; anything to maintain picture and sound. Stylists ceased cutting, curling, bleaching, and teasing, and all talk went silent when so and so was cheating on what's her face or that girl with amnesia was marrying that old guy who used to be her stepdad.

Leila's was a choice gathering spot for The Hens. Typically they tried to book appointments together. This was easily pulled off, because Leila was a longtime sustaining member of The Hens. All of Leila's girls except for Rhonda were also Hens. Rhonda had been employed at Leila's for about five months. She was hired after Carol Reece retired.

Carol Reece had been widowed for about twenty years. When her dearly beloved Buford dearly departed, Carol wailed and screamed and predicted she'd soon die of a broken heart. Once the grips of grief released her, she commenced to look for Buford's replacement. The lady was anything but subtle! She acted like an alley cat in heat anytime a man was around. Carol retired to allow herself more time for prowling around to find a mate. Nothing short of a miracle would have led to Carol meeting a good man. She still hung out at the salon all the time, and no man worth his salt would be caught dead in that place! Anyway, Rhonda moved to Coleman from North Carolina. Nobody knows why she came to Coleman. Surely it wasn't just to work for Leila. What do you want to bet that she thought the goings-on in that place were just crazy? Nobody knew what Rhonda really thought about it. She remained tight lipped. Leila probably made her sign a release not to let any of "The Hens'" secrets escape those tacky walls!

On the second Tuesday of every month Patsy and Ingrid saw Leila to have their coifs dyed, trimmed, and styled within an inch of their lives. By the time Leila was through with them, they'd have enough hairspray for their dos to withstand gale force winds and torrential rains. Some even claimed that Leila used to buy pure back market Teflon and spray her customers' hair with it. Seriously, that was the urban legend that went around Coleman for a long time. Bernadette Calhoun, a long-time loyal patron of Leila's, had a brain tumor. The talk was that a specialist from Duke University said that some sort of toxin had been seeping into her scalp, and it proved to be Teflon sprayed on her hair by Leila. Bernadette survived, and the fact that she started getting her hair done at Curly-Q's added credence to the rumor. Leila probably had access to Teflon because her uncle worked for a plant that made non-stick cookware.

Millie Tate and Jan Brooks usually joined Patsy and Ingrid, but they were getting their colons cleansed. There was a lady on the outskirts of Coleman who did bargain rate colon cleansings in her basement. She didn't have a license to do such procedures, making it an illegal business. It probably amounted to nothing more than a glorified enema. Supposedly, it got rid of toxins, flushing them quickly out of the body and into her septic system. This sort of abrupt ridding of toxins was said to promote a feeling of general well-being. Millie and Jan read about celebrities getting their colons cleansed and felt they must do the same. Those two were like that.

When Princess Diana and Prince Charles got engaged, both of them ordered fake replicas of her ring from a mail-order company. Those gaudy things looked like they came out of a gumball machine, but Millie and Jan thought they were really something because they had the faux "Princess Di Ring." No two women were any fuller of crap than those two. A colon cleansing might have made them lose about fifty pounds a piece. Everybody with a garden should have been lining up at that colon cleansing place with shovels and pick-up trucks to load up all the organic matter that came out of Millie and Jan. It was probably better than cow manure!

While their buddies got their innards uncontaminated, Patsy and Ingrid crucified just about everyone in town. They didn't need a whole lot of evidence to proclaim something as true. A few gifted Hens were psychic and based claims on "funny feelings" they had about people. Other times, The Hens played detective and sloppily compiled their findings to make a case against someones good name.

Patsy wasn't at all happy with her last hair color, so she and Leila discussed a new shade. Judging from the results, her choices must have been; black patent shoes black, midnight blue black, or old crow black. This was the perfect lead in for Patsy to note that she thought Marlene's last hair coloring turned out a little too red and that in addition to the bad hair color, Marlene was putting on a little weight. Patsy's ankles were the size of Marlene's thighs It was just a little odd that she felt at liberty to discuss an extra pound or two on another person. There's a verse in Matthew about noticing the speck in another person's eye while ignoring the beam in your own. Perhaps Patsy had never heard that verse.

Rhonda was doing DeeDee Perkins's hair in the station next to Leila. They were also discussing color, whether or not DeeDee should color, given her condition. DeeDee was a couple of months pregnant. DeeDee's doctor had said that it was okay to have highlights, just not color that had to process in direct contact with the scalp for a long period of time. Rhonda explained that the highlights may come out a different color than they normally would have because of hormonal changes that affect the hair during pregnancy.

Just then, Ingrid pulled a Perry Mason. "Hey, I wonder if that's what's happened with Marlene Prescott's color?"

Patsy joined her fellow super sleuth. "It would all make sense; the hair color, the weight gain, a sudden concern about her finances."

Out of nowhere, Carol popped up behind Patsy's chair to join the conversation. "I got pregnant with my last one when I was about Marlene's age. Ladies in their forties go around thinking they can't get impregnated. That's how those surprise "change of life" babies get here!"

Chapter 6

It was a good thing Marlene was a Christian and a lady, otherwise she would have slapped every one of those Hens right across the face a long time ago. Thankfully fate intervened. Karma came to town one Tuesday afternoon and punched a couple of Hens right between the eyes!

Someone gave the county police an anonymous tip about the illegal colon cleansing place. The police acted quickly because the caller proclaimed that the lady operating the joint was doing a little something extra on the side. The "elixir" she offered patients to relax them before their procedures was actually pure peach moonshine she was making in her backyard. As fate would have it, the bust occurred just as Millie and Jan's colons were being cleansed. So, there they were, lying on metal tables in the woman's basement, tanked up on moonshine, with plastic hoses coming out of their orifices! Detectives from the police department would be making jokes about those posteriors for posterity.

Although Millie and Jan probably wouldn't serve any time in the pokey, they did appear on the local television news and on the front page of the *Coleman Gazette*. The news footage of the colon bust was the best! Millie and Jan had towels over their heads. Like people didn't know who they were! They were so drunk from the moonshine that they had to be carried to the squad cars. It took four big men to carry each of them! After they sobered up, the two were questioned at the station. They tried to portray it like the colon cleansing lady got them drunk and then took advantage of them.

That story was blown to bits when the police found two checks that Millie and Jan had used to pre-pay for their elixirs and cleansings. Jan's check noted "elixir and colon cleansing in the bottom corner." In typical Millie and Jan fashion, their first question for officers was whether or not they could get refunded since they didn't receive the full service they paid for.

Millie spent much of her life in litigation. She had tried to sue half the town. No doubt, she would try to bring a suit against Carla the Colon Cleanser, the police, the media and anyone else she felt had shamed or shorted her in any way.

Millie's daughter Ellie caught trench mouth when she was fourteen. Ellie got it after playing spin-the-bottle at Jenny Bledsoe's party. Millie became bound and determined to get to the bottom of whoever gave her daughter trench mouth and sue them for medical expenses and pain and suffering. She also threatened to sue Jenny Bledsoe's parents for not being better chaperones.

She got Ellie to give her a list of all the boys she kissed. Then, she went to the home of every boy on that list with a pen light and a tongue depressor. Millie marched right up to every one of those boys' homes and demanded to examine their mouths. The parents were so intimidated that they caved and allowed Millie to look in their sons' mouths for signs of the affliction that had struck Ellie. All of the parents, except one.

Millie got a run for her money when she showed up at Jessie Deakins's house. Susie, Jessie's momma, was not a woman to be messed with. You sure didn't want to be on her bad side. Susie told Millie that she'd call the police if she laid a hand on her son. Furthermore, she urged Millie to drop the whole issue. Or else, she'd tell the whole town that precious little Ellie had upped the ante of spin-the-bottle when she decided to play seven minutes in heaven with Brad Benson down in the furnace room of Jennie Bledsoe's house. The matter of Ellie's trench mouth was soon dropped!

News of the colonics raid even reached Marlene's parents in Florida. Marlene's mom called and told her that their whole retirement community thought the story was just hysterical. Marlene's parents were the most popular residents after all the retirees knew about their connection to the illegal colonics solicitors. Marlene's momma was telling all of the ladies in her quilting group that, "It couldn't happen to two more well-deserving ladies. They've shown their butts all their lives. Now, they've just gotten caught!"

It seems that the older people get, the more they become obsessed with their and others' bathroom habits. Marlene's dad got on the phone and complained that Millie and Jan's story opened the flood gates for all the men he hung out with to describe their bowel movements in vivid detail. "We're meeting to play golf this afternoon. I'm half-expecting someone to bring a specimen to show all of us!"

The conversation took a more serious turn when Marlene told them that she talked to Larry McCrumb about how to invest her share from the sale of the farm. Marlene's parents agreed with the advice Larry gave. They had always encouraged Marlene to expand her business. Marlene's momma talked about how proud her Grandma would be to know how Marlene was using her money from their farm.

It was pretty much a done deal at that point. All that was left to do was for her dad to call the guy from the manufacturer who contacted him about the sale. Marlene heard hesitation in her dad's voice when he mentioned finalizing it all. There would be a new chapter in the lives of Marlene and her parents. They hoped it would be a good chapter; full of positive change and new opportunities!

Chapter 7

Charity, Marlene's new employee, began working for her on a Saturday morning. Saturdays had Marlene running around like a chicken with its head cut off. She sold fried pies and coffee to the farmers at the stockyard from seven until nine in the morning. She opened Cutie Pies from ten till three. More often than not, there was a catered event or social for her to deliver pies to on Saturday evenings.

Charity met Marlene at the store around ten. They went over opening and closing procedures and running the cash register. This stuff was old hat for Charity. She had worked in restaurants since the age of sixteen. Next, Marlene showed Charity her pie recipes and asked that she choose a recipe and make it from scratch. This is where Charity really shined. One of the instructors at the technical institute said that Charity was the best pastry student he'd ever had. Marlene decided to turn Charity loose in the kitchen. A little over an hour later, she emerged with a beautiful chocolate chip pecan pie. The crust was perfect: flaky yet tender, golden brown, with a glossy sheen of egg wash. The filling was rich with just the right ratio of chocolate to nuts. The girl obviously knew how to make a pie that was tasty and good to look at. Not only did she make an incredible pie, while the pie was baking, she cleaned the kitchen so thoroughly, that it looked just like it did before she used it. Proficient and efficient; this was the perfect combination of what Marlene was looking for.

Besides being a talented pastry chef and hard worker, Charity was pleasant and intelligent. Marlene had worked by herself for so many years. It was nice to have someone else around. Eventually, Marlene hoped to train Charity to take over some of the paperwork and purchasing aspects of the business.

Charity planned on staying in Coleman for the long haul. Charity's husband was out of state getting his welding certification. Once he was done, there was a good job waiting for him at Tri-County Metals in Coleman. It was the type of job men got into and never left. The wages were great, and the benefits couldn't be beat. Charity and her husband were a couple of small town kids who had found their dream. They looked forward to a simple life, working and living in Coleman. Charity could easily have landed a job as a pastry chef in a fancy big city restaurant, but neither of them wanted any part of the city life.

* * *

Charity's first week of working for Marlene went superbly. Marlene invited Charity to have dinner with her, Allison, and Dorothy. They decided to eat at Bobby's Café. Fortunately, the food was excellent, because there really wasn't anywhere else to eat a sit-down meal in Coleman. The only other restaurant was Sally's Drive In. It was great for burgers, pizzas and ice cream, but it was strictly a drive through.

As usual, Bobby's was busy. Thankfully Marlene and her cohorts were seated in the corner for the evening. If one got seated in the middle of Bobby's everyone stopped to talk to them. Sometimes it was fun to catch up with all the other "Colemanites," but that night the girls just wanted to chat.

Unfortunately, they ran smack dab into Shira Conner as they started to sit down. Amongst friends, they had changed Shira Conner's name to "Sugar Coater." Whatever the situation,

Shira would put a pretty face on it. Her glass was perpetually half full. Lemons were always being made into lemonade, and that frown had to always be turned upside down. In the war of Hens versus Non-Hens, Shira was Switzerland. She maintained a perfectly neutral stance. Shira was sweet and completely annoying. In theory, everyone should have strived to be more like Shira; but all that positive energy was like nails on a chalkboard. Sometimes, things were just bad and one had to acknowledge it! Her life was going to Hell in a hand basket, and she didn't even realize it. Shira told that her father was "enjoying a restful retirement." Her mother was "keeping busy with her hobbies." Her husband was "cutting back on his hours at work to spend more time with her and the kids," and her children were "both just full of personality." All the while, Shira had a glazed over look of pure delirium.

Now, if one were to have ripped off Shira's rose-colored glasses and filled her Prozac bottle with a placebo, here's what was really going on: Her lazy alcoholic father sat in his Lazy Boy recliner everyday and guzzled beer until he passed out. Shira's mom spent all day down in their musty old basement filling bowls with potpourri and gluing seashells to stuff just to avoid being upstairs with her drunk husband. Kendall, Shira's husband, lied on his last time sheet and was not allowed to work any overtime. Both of Shira's children bounced off the walls twenty-four/seven. They suffered from hyperactivity disorder, but Shira preferred to think of them as "spirited." After Shira bade them an all-to-cheerful ado, Dorothy rolled her eyes and the four ladies settled in to converse.

This was Dorothy and Allison's first time meeting Charity. From all that they'd heard about her, expectations were high and Charity exceeded them. Charity just could not have been any more endearing. The girl was only about five feet tall and one-hundred pounds soaking wet. Her thick blond hair hung in a swingy chin-length bob. Charity had a face like a little China doll. Her eyes were blue and cat-like. She had a tiny turned up nose and full lips. Her coloring was fair with rosy apple cheeks. Charity told them that she was twenty-four. As far as her looks went, she could have easily passed for a teenager. At the same time, she possessed a maturity and confidence that made her seem very wise for her years. She was from West Virginia, but her husband grew up about fifteen minutes outside of Coleman. He was a star running back for Blue Mountain High School. Everyone thought Joe would get a scholarship until he blew out his right knee in the last five minutes of the final game of his senior year. It was a heartbreaker for football fans all around those parts.

The two met when Joe and some of his buddies were on a deer hunting trip in West Virginia. At the time, Charity was working as a waitress in a restaurant where Joe and his friends ate breakfast every morning. On the fourth day of their seven day stay, Joe asked Charity to join him for dinner that evening. For the last two days of the trip, Joe didn't even hunt with his friends. He wanted to spend every moment he could with the pretty little West Virginia gal. After Joe went home the two wrote and talked on the phone constantly. Pretty soon, Joe was driving to West Virginia every weekend. He proposed one year after they met and they'd been married for a year and a half.

It was amazing how quickly Charity felt at ease with them. Marlene, Dorothy and Allison thought being around Charity was like having a little sister. After about ten or fifteen minutes of getting to know each other Charity said that she had something important to share with them. "You guys have to promise not to breathe this to a soul, but I'm just going to explode if I can't tell someone my good news. I'm going to have a baby! I haven't been to the doctor yet, but I've taken three pregnancy tests and they've all been positive. I don't want to tell Joe until he gets home from his training and I know he will want to be with me when I tell our families. So, you three are the only ones who know. I just don't want this to get around. I've heard women in Coleman can be a little gossipy."

"Oh you don't have to tell us!" Marlene replied. "We can tell you exactly the ones to watch out for."

The three quickly gave Charity a tutorial on The Hens; how to identify one, which ones were the worst, and how they operated. Allison added, "If I were you, I'd drive over to Langrid and go to Dr. Bates. Ken Finney is the only doctor in Coleman who delivers babies. Three Hens work for him. As soon as you call to make an appointment, everyone in town will know your condition. Every ovarian cyst, venereal disease, and pregnancy that Dr. Finney treats is broadcasted by The Hens. If you go to Dr. Finney, you might as well tell the Tri-County News to put it on their six o'clock edition."

Allison proceeded to tell Charity a story about an incident involving Dr. Finney and an almost lawsuit. Corrine DelRay used to live in Coleman. It was a good thing Corrine was beautiful because she was dumber than a dang coal bucket. "Looks don't need books," is what she used to say when she was in school.

At an early age, it was instilled in Corrine that she should settle down with a rich man. Corrine aspired to be a kept woman and didn't think there was anything derogatory about the term "trophy wife." Corrine's mama taught her that because Corrine sure wasn't smart enough to take care of herself.

When Corrine was about twenty-one, she turned the head of Bruce Wilson. Bruce's grandfather was the founder of Tri County Metals. Bruce was many years older than Corrine and really nothing to look at. Still, he was rich as could be, and that was all Corrine cared about. So, dumb as a coal bucket, but shiny as a new penny, Corrine, and sharp as a tack, but plain as white bread, Bruce, became Coleman's premier couple.

After a few months of courting, Bruce made a heartfelt public proposal during the Coleman Annual Fourth of July Fireworks

Display. Tri County Metals paid for the event, so Bruce could do just about whatever he wanted to. After all the fireworks had been shot, Bruce awkwardly stepped onto the center podium and told the whole town of his undying love for Corrine. He asked her to join him on the podium, where he slid a diamond the size of a gumball on her finger.

As an engagement present, Bruce flew Corrine and her sister to Paris. He turned her loose with his credit cards, telling her to find a designer wedding gown, lingerie for their honeymoon and anything else she wanted. Well, Corrine found an exquisite hand-beaded gown, lots of lacy French lingerie, and a brooding poet named Pierre. Nobody actually knew his name, but everyone referred to him as Pierre. Chances were pretty good that he was named Pierre or Jean Claude. Most French men seem to have feathery names like that.

It seems that Corrine became pretty cozy with Pierre. A few days after returning from Paris, she had a pre-wedding appointment with Dr. Finney. Corrine came out of her appointment with two prescriptions. One was for birth control pills and the other for an antibiotic. Seems Pierre had been pleasuring more than a few young, nubile, wide-eyed American ladies in the romantic city of Paris. In the interest of being polite, let's just say that Pierre gave Corrine a social disease, but not one that you can contract by shaking hands.

Corrine's plan was to clear up her condition with the antibiotic and never speak a word to anyone of her tawdry encounter in a foreign land. Her plan was foiled by Wanda Carlson. Wanda was Dr. Finney's head nurse and happened to be sitting in on Corrine's exam. One would think that Wanda's duties as a nurse would have trumped any desire to share confidential information with The Hens, but The Hens were sort of like family and families share secrets.

Wanda told Britta Briggs. Britta told Angela Patrick and Angela told everyone! It took about two days for Bruce to find out.

A bewildered and devastated Bruce nixed the nuptials, and took back the ring and the dress. All Corrine got to keep was the skimpy lingerie. Bruce would have taken that back too, until he imagined that Corrine had probably worn it for Pierre. He sold the wedding dress and ring, but knew that second-hand lingerie has no resale value. Even during his most terrible crisis, Bruce kept his business wits about him.

With her hopes of marrying a rich man dashed, Corrine hired an attorney and filed a lawsuit against Dr. Finney for violating her rights as a patient. The suit was for a huge amount that if awarded, would have taken his practice under. Corrine reasoned that she should receive the amount needed to set her up in the lifestyle she would have enjoyed had her marriage come to fruition.

Dr. Finney's attorney offered a hefty settlement. The offer became attractive when Corrine realized that, if the case made it to court, everyone would have to hear about her condition she contracted in France. Actually, everyone already did know, but Corrine was hugely unaware of it as she was oblivious to most things. She took the settlement and left town.

Dr. Finney fired Wanda and brought in attorneys to conduct several training sessions with his employees. They were told about patients' rights and professional behavior. Each employee was made to sign a contract stating that violation of any ethical or professional code would result in immediate dismissal. An ethics board investigated Dr. Finney, but found that he had not personally committed any wrongs.

For a while, Dr. Finney's staff walked a narrow and straight line, guided by ethics, consideration for patients, and professionalism. Over time, some Hens began re-gaining important positions in his practice. Before long his office was again contaminated with Hens. From billing, to the nurses, to the after hours cleaning service, that place was full of them. His office had more leaks than the Titanic!

As for Bruce, his story had a happy ending. He met the love of his life about a year after he broke things off with Corrine. She was a sweet, but rather ordinary looking girl who fell in love with Bruce and not his money.

When they got engaged, he gave her an even bigger ring than he'd given Corrine and sent her to London for a bridal shopping excursion. This time, Bruce accompanied his fiancé on her overseas adventure.

Last anyone had heard, Corrine and her mama got this two-for-one deal on old rich guys. After Corrine's father passed, she and her mama used his life insurance money to buy a condo on the coast in North Carolina. Corrine's mother and father had not shared the same domicile for many years, but they never bothered with getting a divorce. That meant Corrine's mom was still entitled to everything when he passed. They met these brothers who ran a bunch of those Calabash style seafood buffets. Corrine and her mama each got a big four bedroom beach house plus they had all-you-can-eat crab legs every night. Their lives became all about cash, flash and Calabash.

Marlene switched the subject. She had some news, too. It was not as important or exciting as Charity's pregnancy, but big new nonetheless. Marlene lit up as she talked about her plans to purchase the building next door and expand her business. She was hoping to have an eat-in area for customers. Her menu would not change much except that she wanted to offer a wide selection of gourmet coffees and teas. She also hoped to have a section of shelving in which she would put newspapers, magazines and books on local history and landmarks. Along one wall, Marlene wanted to have a couple of computers and then a couple of more tables with wireless access. She envisioned a nice coffee shop atmosphere where people of all ages could hang out, read, or work.

Marlene worried that plans for expansion so soon after Charity had begun working at Cutie Pies might frighten Charity, but she seemed almost as excited about it as Marlene. The next day, Marlene would take the first step towards making her vision a reality. She was prepared to make her offer on the building next door.

Chapter 8

Heeding Allison's advice, Charity saw Dr. Bates to have her pregnancy confirmed. The most exciting part of the visit was when Dr. Bates let her listen to the baby's heartbeat. It was a good steady beat. The baby was thriving!

Charity met Rena McAllister in Dr. Bates's waiting room. Rena had never met a stranger, and nobody had ever met anyone stranger than Rena. She had a dire need to share her deepest darkest secrets with everyone. It was a shame she hadn't joined The Hens. That was the one group of ladies that would have relished listening to her stories about how she'd been wronged and deceived by men, was neglected as a child and was still afraid to sleep without a night light. Rena liked peanut butter, hated blueberries and called in sick to work when Marie Osmond was going to be selling dolls on the TV shopping channel. She had O-negative blood, gave blood once, but passed out, had her first kiss when she was fifteen and had worn the same pair of house shoes for ten years. Anyone who ever had the unfortunate luck of being behind her in a grocery store line knew all this about her. Now, because she was in a waiting room with her for five minutes, Charity knew it too.

Charity got her pre-natal vitamins at a pharmacy in Langrid. Although no Hens worked at Coleman Pharmacy, it seemed like there was always one or two in there perusing. Coleman

Pharmacy was the only place in town to buy Aqua Net Hairspray, blue Maybelline eye shadow and support panty hose; three fundamentals of Hen fashion.

As soon as Charity got back from Langrid and filled Marlene in on her appointment, Marlene went next door. The adjoining building had a big "For Sale" sign in the window with a number to call. The sign was now gone. She called the real estate office that had listed the property and found out that it was sold the day before.

Marlene's best hope was that someone who planned to fix the property up bought it and would resell it or rent it out. That was her only hope of getting the space for expansion. She called Harriet Squibb to see if she knew anything. Harriet worked at the courthouse and knew about most of the property transfers in the county. All Harriet knew was that a gentleman bought the property and that nobody seemed to know his plans for the building.

Marlene was near despair when she called Dorothy. "I'm kicking myself! If I had just called about the space sooner, it would be mine. Oh well, maybe it's just not meant to be."

Dorothy tried to encourage Marlene. "You're not sure that this mystery man is going to keep the building. Maybe he'll do all the renovations that you wouldn't want to fool with anyway, then turn around, and sell it in a few months."

Marlene was perplexed by who the buyer could be. When the sale was final, it would become public knowledge; but Marlene would have really liked to have known the buyer's identity sooner. She bet The Hens knew something about this man! They knew everything going on in town. If Dorothy listened carefully to Patsy's phone conversations at work, she maybe could find out what Marlene needed to know!

Although she had a fabulous life that she was content with, those close to her thought Marlene sometimes wished she had a child. "It's just not the way my life has worked out," was her answer when anyone asked why she never married and had a family.

When someone had a baby, she got so excited. You'd think it was she who was becoming a new mom. After many years of trying, Dorothy and her husband, Tom, had been unsuccessful in having a child. After spending a king's ransom on fertility treatments, they were in the process of trying to adopt. Marlene had been there for Dorothy in every way. Marlene had been a shoulder to cry on and spent countless hours helping Dorothy research adoption agencies. She had even offered to help finance travel expenses if Dorothy and Tom had to go overseas to adopt.

Marlene planned to go over to Langrid that night to do some shopping. They had the only mall within an hour of Coleman. She was out of foundation and was using that as her excuse. "I can't go to work tomorrow without my foundation. I'll be so pale. People will think I'm sick!"

What she really wanted to do was get a baby present for Charity. She would be on her way to the makeup counter and "just happen to see" something and buy it for Charity. The day after Allison had announced her first pregnancy, Marlene had gone on a wild shopping spree, and had come back with bags full of blankets, bibs, and cuddly toys.

Dorothy was going to go with her, but her husband needed assistance. Tom had a photography business and was going to be working at Gretchen Harlow's wedding that weekend. He and Dorothy were going over to the church and the country club to figure out the set up and lighting for the ceremony and reception.

At the make-up counter, Marlene ran into Kelly Nielson. Kelly was an interesting character. To look at her, you'd think she grew up in a wigwam, not a cozy brick Cape Cod with a wraparound porch on Main Street. When she was in the fourth grade, Kelly did a school project on genealogy. Through her research, Kelly discovered that her great-grandmother was half Cherokee Indian. She didn't uncover anything new. Her mother had always known about their Native American heritage. Kelly's mom never made a big deal over it because most people around Coleman had some Native American ancestry. Kelly really identified with her Cherokee lineage. Suddenly, she was wearing her hair in two braids and dressing in faux buckskins. Kelly's parents thought it would just be a phase but it stuck. Kelly still celebrated her heritage, favoring long braids, turquoise jewelry, and playing ceremonial beats on a tom-tom out in her yard. A few neighbors and all of The Hens accused her of smoking a little illegal substance in her peace pipe while she was out there in her yard. Someone anonymously called the police on her last year. They examined the contents of the pipe only to find that it was full of legal medicinal herbs.

Sometimes, Kelly even took to wearing war paint. Apparently, she used red Elizabeth Arden lip color and not pokeberries to make those red stripes on her cheeks. Kelly also picked up some matching red nail polish at the Arden counter. Seems she was going to one of those gambling casinos in Cherokee, North Carolina that weekend and hoped to meet some Indian fellow.

Kelly was bound and determined that she would only procreate with a full blooded Native American as not to water down her already compromised bloodline. Once in high school, Glen asked her out on a date. She responded "I will only date red men."

If she were looking for redneck men, there would have been plenty to choose from. As far as full-blooded Native American, her pool of eligibles in the immediate area was slim pickens. Though many in Coleman had Native American ancestors, most began intermarrying long ago. With any luck, Cherokee, North Carolina would provide her the opportunity to find a man who met her very specific criteria.

Incidentally, Kelly inspired one of Marlene's most creative and delicious pies. After one of her visits to an Indian reservation, Kelly brought Marlene some traditional Native American recipes. Marlene was always telling people to bring her recipes that they would like to see made into a pie. Marlene took the recipe for Indian Fry Bread and the one for Indian pudding and made an Indian pudding pie with a fry bread crust. The filling was made with yellow cornmeal, molasses, spices and raisins. It was an especially popular pie in the fall. Many Thanksgiving tables in Coleman would not have been complete without it.

Fortunately, Kelly had been able to parlay her passion for all things Cherokee into a career. She'd always had a talent for the arts. Kelly did beautiful paintings and sculptures depicting Native American life. As a service to the community, she gave free lectures on the Cherokee history and culture and encouraged young people to be good stewards of the environment. Kids at the elementary school loved her. She painted their faces and taught them ceremonial dances.

After Marlene got her foundation from the makeup counter, she headed over to the baby department. Bibs and socks would be useful no matter if it was a boy or girl, so that's what Marlene decided on. Once Charity found out the baby's gender, Marlene could do some serious baby clothes shopping. Alas, Marlene was met by DeeDee who was selecting items for her baby registry. Marlene started to explain herself before recalling that, for a while, mums would be the word on Charity's pregnancy. Marlene told DeeDee that she was getting gifts for a friend. Such nondescript information raised suspicions in DeeDee's mind.

The next day, DeeDee had a hair appointment. She shared the previous night's encounter and the ladies of Leila's became all a twitter. Their beady eyes lit up as they came to the realization that they had proof of their suspicions. "Oh she has to be! I wonder whose it is! I had a feeling she was trampin' around town!"

Just so happened that Charlotte was getting her hair done next to DeeDee. Charlotte never had totally gotten over her prom night heartbreak. It didn't help that she had never given up on Glen's being her knight in shining armor. Charlotte still lived with her parents and Glen's parents still were across the street. From time-to-time, she'd go over and talk to Glen when he visited. Rather than becoming discouraged with each year that passed, Charlotte felt that the chance of their becoming a couple got greater with time. She reasoned that since he hadn't married yet, he must have been holding out for something! Charlotte told The Hens "If he'd stop thinking about that Marlene, Glen would be all mine!"

Charlotte knew he went to Cutie Pies every Friday afternoon. "He buys his pies from that little tart!" is what Charlotte liked to say.

Last time he went to see his parents; Glen was carrying a pie that had similar ingredients to a red velvet cake. The top was covered in a thick, white, cream cheese topping. Cutting into it revealed a filling that was scarlet red, flavored with cocoa, buttermilk and a touch of vinegar.

Marlene named the pie The Scarlet Lady. "That pie's suggestive and cheap, just like the woman who created it" ranted Charlotte. "I can't believe Glen even took it into his parents' home. Just think. It sits there in that pie case alongside those peach and apple pies that Marlene's grandmother taught her to make. That sweet old lady would have never come up with a pie named Scarlet Lady! I bet she'd be so disappointed in Marlene."

Charlotte's first thought was that she couldn't wait to tell Glen that Marlene was pregnant. Surely that would kill any interest he had in her. Then Charlotte was overcome with a horrible thought! What if the baby was the fruit of Glen's loins! "Maybe he's getting more than pies from that little tart every Friday afternoon!"

Charlotte and DeeDee spent the next couple of hours making predictions about the supposed father of Marlene's supposed baby.

Dorothy was still trying to help Marlene by listening in on Patsy's calls. No luck, she didn't hear any mention of who may have purchased the building next to Cutie Pies.

As much as Dorothy hated to do it, she was going to ask Patsy if she knew anything. Dorothy feared she would trigger a round of twenty questions and a load of speculations, but she was on a search for information and Patsy was her best hope. In the realm of town chit-chat, Patsy was like an encyclopedia. She probably couldn't recall what she had for breakfast that morning, but she could go back in her brain and pull out the menu that Ingrid prepared for the Canasta Club's Spring Brunch five years ago and tell what everybody there was wearing.

"Hey Patsy, I was wondering. Have you heard anything about who bought that old building beside Cutie Pies? Someone was telling Marlene that a gentleman purchased it this week. I was just wondering if someone's putting in a new business there."

Patsy told Dorothy that she hadn't heard anything and acted quite disinterested with the whole matter. Dorothy knew that underneath that blasé reaction Patsy was really wondering why Marlene and Dorothy cared who had bought the business. Dorothy hardly ever asked her anything.

Once back at her desk, Patsy got to work. Her first call was to Charlotte. Since Charlotte's mom worked downtown, she figured they might have heard something. "No Patsy, I don't know who bought it. Speaking of Cutie Pies, did you know Marlene Prescott is pregnant? Now, don't quote me on it. I don't want my name involved in some big stink, but I've heard from a very reliable source that she's expecting."

Chapter 9

There was a bit of a dilemma when the decision had to be made whether or not to serve alcohol at Gretchen Harlow's and Keith Mann's wedding. Gretchen's family on her mother's side was made up of teetotalers who abstained from drinking and, for the most part, people and establishments that promoted or condoned it. Keith's family felt that there was nothing wrong with a little drinking as long as there was some upholding of moderation and control. Gretchen's father's philosophy was, "If it's there, I'll drink it."

Rarely was it there for him. Gretchen's mom didn't allow alcohol to be brought into their home or consumed in her presence. So, Mr. Harlow only had a drink when, on rare occasion, Mrs. Harlow allowed him to go camping with his brothers. Once, she found a leftover beer in his cooler after a camping trip; and she made bread with it. That's the only time she ever used alcohol.

Keith's family, at first, wanted to have an open bar, and even offered to pay for it, even though the bill for the reception traditionally belonged to the bride's family. Gretchen's mom was offended by the mere mention of having an unlimited flow of alcohol at her daughter's wedding. Gretchen's father tried to urge her mother to ease up a little for this one occasion. He even suggested that a little glass of bubbly on her daughter's wedding day might help to calm her nerves, allowing her (and him) to actually enjoy the festivities.

At last, a compromise was reached. They decided to serve champagne punch and not tell Gretchen's mom about it. The spiked punch was in a silver bowl; so that there was no blatant reminder that alcohol was on the premises. Just to avoid confusion or any accidental consumption, Julie Young, the alcoholic punch server, alerted people that there was a little champagne in the silver punch bowl. Those who didn't want any alcohol were directed to the next table where there was a crystal bowl full of pink lemonade and a pitcher of ice water with lemons floating in it. Clarence Salyers claimed to have not heard Julie say that the silver bowl had alcoholic punch in it, but he finished his cup anyway and appeared to be going for seconds.

Of all the weddings Tom had photographed, this one made him the most nervous. Gretchen was the only girl from Coleman to ever win the title of Miss Virginia. Sadly, the picture that made it to all the newspapers in the state was completely unflattering.

Gretchen was a beautiful girl. She managed to look pageant prepped even when she was just grocery shopping in Coleman. Her makeup was always flawless and fresh, her hair was bouncy and full, and her outfits always looked like they came straight from a Neiman Marcus Catalog. Not an easy thing to do, since there was not a Neiman's within five hundred miles of Coleman!

The thing about Gretchen; as fine-looking as she was, Gretchen was a very unsightly crier. Now some girls can cry pretty and others just can't. While this isn't such a problem for the average girl, it's a tragic flaw for a pageant contestant. Every pageant winner, from Miss America to Miss Okra Festival has to do the obligatory cry. It's just expected. Why it's half the reason people love to watch pageants! Few things are more moving than watching a beauty queen take that walk she's dreamed of all her life, waving to her adoring audience, mouthing "I love you!" to her family, all while crying that pretty cry.

A pretty cry is a little tear trickling down one's cheek while the rest of the face is undisturbed. An ugly cry is a red faced sob, quivering lips, and a runny nose. Add two inches of makeup being washed away and you'd have Gretchen on pageant night.

Some photographer got her about three minutes into the crying. By that time, she was puffy, snotty, and hyperventilating. The picture made every paper in the state and became Virginia's favorite joke. When Gretchen made her mandatory public appearances, she was heckled mercilessly. For a whole year parade watchers and school children mocked her.

The next year, when she had to relinquish her crown, Gretchen vowed she would not cry; but she did, because Gretchen was a very weepy girl. She took her final lap down the runway as her pre-recorded speech personally thanked just about everyone whom she'd ever met. She also thanked others whom she'd never met, but who'd inspired her. Needless to say, that speech was lengthy!

For the first half of the speech, Gretchen bit her lip and held the tears back. Then the dam broke! An explosion of tears came. It was a forceful, full body cry, much worse than when she won the title. She was shaking and couldn't catch her breath. Gretchen was advised to tuck a little tissue in her cleavage in anticipation of the big cry, but she didn't. She was almost forced to wipe her nose on her sash until a stage hand stepped up on the stage with a box of tissues. What did the photographer capture from that night? You guessed it, Gretchen's big ugly cry. A four by six shot of her ran right under a five by seven shot of the new winner in every paper in the state!

With one's wedding day, hopefully, being more emotional than one's pageant days, there was some major apprehension about "Cry-Baby Bride" breaking down. Tom played the role of photographer/therapist and it worked like a charm. Whenever he noticed Gretchen starting to tear up, he started telling a silly joke or funny story. It was sort of like when Tom photographed little kids and had all these funny props to make them laugh.

Besides supporting her husband's efforts, Dorothy had another reason that she was rooting for Gretchen to hang in there and stay tear free. Patsy and some other Hens stood to gain financially if Gretchen broke down. Dorothy said that Patsy stayed on the phone all week at the office. She was putting together a betting pool on how many minutes of her wedding ceremony Gretchen could go without shedding a tear.

Organizing the betting pool had Patsy putting in the hardest day's work Dorothy had ever seen from her. She even made a spread sheet on her computer to show all the women in the pool and the stipulations of their bets. Dorothy walked by her desk and just happened to glance at the spread sheet.

At the top of the list was Gladys Hoover. Gladys held a grudge against Gretchen ever since her daughter competed against Gretchen and lost in the "Little Miss Coleman Heritage Days," back when the girls were in elementary school. Her daughter, Bethany, was a right cute girl, but not really the pageant type. Bethany had always been more tomboy than glamour queen.

Gladys used to be quite attractive, on the outside anyway. Her attitude had always been ugly as sin. She pretended to be pleasant long enough to convince the judges that she deserved the title of "Miss Coleman" when she was a young woman.

Gladys still went on about it like she had won Miss Universe or something. Her looks had gone so downhill that strangers didn't even believe her when she told them she was a former beauty queen. It was amazing that the fact she was a former beauty queen ever came up with strangers, but Gladys somehow managed to work it into all her conversations.

Like Election Day, when Gladys was in line to vote in the local primary elections, the woman in front of Gladys had just moved to Coleman. Gladys was saying, "I think it's great that you're already taking an interest in local politics. When I was Miss Coleman, I spent most of my reign campaigning for positive change in this town. I thought it was my civic duty to use my title to influence local citizens and leaders."

Yeah right! The only thing political she got involved with was Clancy Thomas, who was on the school board. Clancy and Gladys carried on like a couple of rabbits until Clancy's girlfriend caught them going at it in his car. Clancy's girlfriend put an end to the relationship by threatening to tell the commission reigning over the Miss America pageant system, for which Miss Coleman was a primary.

Talk about civic duty, Clancy's girlfriend would have done the whole town a service by keeping Gladys from competing in the Miss Virginia pageant. She was just a black eye on Coleman! Literally, she twirled a baton for her talent and blacked her eye when she tossed the baton and it came down on her face. You had to give one thing to Gladys. She hung in there and finished the twirling routine despite the painful injury and swelling about her face.

Then, there was her answer in the interview competition. Her question was "What Virginian do you think has made the biggest contribution to this country?" The question was so easy! George Washington, Thomas Jefferson, Patrick Henry, the list of people she could have talked about was endless.

The answer Gladys gave was worse than stupid. It was irrelevant. Perhaps she thought the emcee asked the same question she'd gotten in the Miss Coleman pageant, because Gladys gave the exact same response. Her question for the Miss Coleman interview was "Who has had the biggest influence in your life?" Gladys's answer in both pageants was; "My mother, because she was a good example for me and my siblings and showed her family unconditional love."

The answer was sweet (if a little too simplistic) and even appropriate for the question posed at the Miss Coleman pageant.

Everyone at the Miss Virginia pageant was left with a collective "What the heck?" One gentleman in the audience used an expletive that was a bit more colorful.

Gladys petitioned the pageant commission to reconsider her scores. She asserted that neither the baton beating nor flubbing her interview questions was her own fault. Gladys called a press conference, although there were really only two newspaper reporters that attended. "The stage lights were going brighter than they had in rehearsals. That blinded me and I could not see my baton when I tossed it up. When the host asked my interview question, feedback from the sound system made his words difficult for me to understand."

Those were Gladys's explanations for her faux pas. The head of the pageant commission's reply was succinct. "A Miss Virginia must be prepared for the unexpected during all public appearances. Unexpected occurrences must be handled with the utmost grace and dignity. As the governing board of the Miss Virginia, USA Pageant, we do not feel that you handled your setbacks in the best way possible."

Gladys continued in her protest, threatening to sue. That forced the judges to reveal her scores. Even if her talent and interview portion had gone perfectly, there would have still been no chance of her winning or even placing in the pageant. She did not impress the judges in her private interview; her posture was bad; and she didn't perform the mandatory quarter turns in the swimsuit competition. Everyone thought she left out the quarter turns because her butt was so flat. Who wants to turn their flat behind towards an audience of thousands? Regardless, it would have been numerically impossible for Gladys to have clinched the crown or even a trophy in the pageant. That was the end of Gladys's press conference and her pageant career.

Gladys tried to push Bethany into pageants to give herself a do-over. If Gladys couldn't push past Coleman in the pageant world, maybe her offspring could. No matter how much Gladys and her husband spent on frilly dresses, dance lessons and even a private pageant coach, little Bethany just wouldn't be converted into a pageant girl.

The worst thing was watching Bethany clog for the talent portions. Bethany's displeasure for being on stage would be written all over her face. Her moves were fine. She could clog fast and was always right on beat with the music. Gladys would have her in some Lycra and sequined get-up with huge ribbons in her tap shoes and braided Pippi Longstocking pigtails. Before she'd go out, Gladys would give her a pep talk and end it with, "Sparkle and shine!"

The only sparkling and shining was from her sequined costume. Bethany looked really cute, but the poor child would be up there clogging her heart out with all the joy and passion of a girl who had someone holding a gun to her head saying, "Dance girl or I'll shoot your brains out!"

It was painful to watch and many refused by looking away, reading their pageant programs, or going to the restroom. Some even considered it child abuse.

Gladys once even resorted to sabotage. Bethany was a reluctant contestant in the "Little Miss Virginia State Fair." In the room where all the contestants were getting ready, Gladys plugged in a steam humidifier. She hid it under a table and did it so discreetly that nobody noticed until all the girls' hair begin to frizz. Curls and tears fell as mortified little girls and their moms tried to salvage the wrecked hairstyles and frayed nerves. The moms worked in triage mode, wielding hairbrushes, curlers, bobby pins and spray; but, alas, nothing could salvage the springy ringlets that were so coveted in the world of tiny tot pageants.

When the humidifier was discovered, Gladys was thought to be the culprit because Bethany was the only contestant who wasn't there. Bethany had been under the weather that week. Gladys urged Bethany and her husband to stay back at the hotel room for an extra hour so that Bethany could get a little more rest. Gladys assured them she'd get Bethany's dressing area all set up so that she could get ready quickly once she got to the auditorium.

All the other moms ganged up on Gladys when the humidifier was discovered. In her defense, she said that Bethany was sick and she thought she needed to run the humidifier for an hour before Bethany's arrival so that the air quality would be suitable. Bethany still didn't win, but she did have the best hair.

When Bethany was a teenager, Gladys used to bring salty snacks like chips and crackers and put them out in the contestants' dressing area on dress rehearsal night. It seemed like a sweet gesture, but it was pure evil. Everyone knew those girls starved themselves for weeks before the pageant. Bethany didn't have to resort to dieting because she was naturally thin and so active in athletics.

Hungry and suffering from pageant stress, those girls would scarf Gladys's devious snacks. You know how it is with chips. You can't eat just one. The night after the salt laden dress rehearsals would be the actual pageant night. As Gladys hoped, several contestants retained fluid from all the salt they'd eaten, making their gowns tight and their faces bloated. Even then, Bethany only secured a third place trophy and a gift certificate for ten free tanning sessions.

After a few years, they gave up and let her do her own thing. Even though Bethany became a lovely, well-adjusted young lady, who attended college on a softball scholarship and graduated with honors, Gladys was still bitter that her daughter never won a crown. Actually, Bethany did win Homecoming Princess in the tenth grade, but Gladys didn't count that because it was voted on by high school students rather than pageant judges. At least she did support Bethany by attending all her softball games and yelling, "Sparkle and shine!" whenever Bethany was up to bat.

With each call Patsy made regarding the betting pool, she tried to find out if anyone knew any information on who had purchased the building beside Marlene. She came up with nothing! Not even The Hens, who practically knew what everyone in town had for dinner last night, knew a thing about this mysterious gentleman.

Chapter 10

Victory! Victory! Gretchen reigned victorious over The Hens and their silly little betting pool! She got through the entire ceremony without a tear. Her eyes never even glistened. Patsy was so aggravated that she put so much work into the futile betting pool. While walking out of the sanctuary Patsy was saying "Gretchen seemed sort of detached and unemotional if you ask me. I probably shouldn't say this, but I don't give that marriage much chance of lasting!"

Patsy liked to preface a malicious statement with, "I probably shouldn't say this, but . . . " She should have just not said it! Monday, she would probably start organizing a pool on when Gretchen would file for divorce.

The reception was a girls' night out for Dorothy, Allison and Marlene. Allison's daughter was sick with the chicken pox. Her husband Gary, who hated going to weddings, quickly volunteered to stay home with the kids. It was sort of fun for them to get all dressed up and hang out on a Saturday night.

They noticed that Gina Herndan was casing the place. Gina was a kleptomaniac, but she didn't steal anything that could get her thrown in jail. If there was a container of sugar packets on a restaurant table, Gina dumped them in her purse. Whenever Gina wrote a check, she borrowed a pen, and then kept it. The bank had their pens chained to the counter to avoid theft. Gina claimed that the counter pen was out of ink so she could steal the teller's pen. Friends of hers received shampoos and soaps from hotel rooms as gifts. That basket of lollipops the bank sat out for children, Gina helped herself to three or four. Allison's kids swore that Gina gave out stolen bank lollipops for Halloween. Since the reception featured a buffet, Gina would surely take enough food with her to make a nice supper for next evening. Others stared in disbelief as she removed a plastic food storage container from her pocket book and dumped her plate of Swedish meatballs into it. Gina's husband was an insurance underwriter. He was all about the bottom line and cutting costs. Instead of being embarrassed by her behavior, he found it endearing. When he told of how they met, he claimed that she "just stole my heart." Why not, she stole everything else!

Tom was put in a precarious position when Gina and her husband wanted him to do a photo of them for their twenty-fifth anniversary. As always, she tried to find a way to get something without paying. "Why don't you do our photographs for free? In exchange, we'll sign a release allowing you to use them for advertisements. It's a win/win for all of us!"

What made them think their pictures would be so good that Tom would want to use them as advertisement? He was a great photographer, but he couldn't work miracles. Instead of telling them that they weren't photogenic enough for an advertisement, Tom was diplomatic and told them that all of his customers had to pay a sitting fee and that he did offer some discount packages, but nothing for free. They left, but not before telling Tom that he ought to rethink their offer. "I'll call you if I change my mind" he told them.

Tom never called and they wound up doing their own anniversary photo using a tripod set up in their living room. The picture wasn't too bad of them. What they neglected to notice before having it put in the newspaper was their house dog in the background, lifting his leg and peeing on a ficus tree in the corner.

There was a bit of an uproar from some offended newspaper subscribers. The "Special Features" editor swore that he did not notice the dog in the background before letting the photo run. The only solution was to re-run the photo without the dog relieving himself in the background. Gina and her husband were too cheap to pay for having another photo developed. Instead, they cut out a picture of the dog in a doggy sweater and had it glued over the offensive shot. In the first photo, the dog was in the distance. The second photo was a close-up of their dog. The dog in their doctored picture wasn't exactly to scale with the rest the picture. So, what ran was a picture of them with a giant Yorky in a bright red sweater. The dog was at least two feet from where they were sitting, but was taller than them. The caption should have read "Couple gets attacked by giant Yorkshire Terrier."

As the girls sipped on a little champagne punch, Millie walked by Marlene and said, "Hasn't your doctor told you to stay away from that stuff?"

Allison quickly responded, "Oh this isn't the strong stuff. We don't touch moonshine."

"It was elixir!" Millie screeched as she stomped off in a huff.

Marlene and Dorothy couldn't believe Allison said that, but they were glad she did. As the three of them laughed and enjoyed the night The Hens noticed that Marlene was getting a second cup of champagne punch.

Odder than The Hens behavior was that of Glen Davis. Allison joked, "Here comes your sweetheart, Marlene," as Glen got up to get more pigs-in-a-blanket from the buffet table.

In a truly surprising move, Glen did not even look at Marlene. He totally ignored her! Marlene was both relieved and befuddled by Glen's oblivion. "He didn't come by to get a pie yesterday. He never misses a Friday afternoon. I thought he might be sick or something. Hopefully, he's decided to move on. I just hate to lose a good customer!"

In a very unsubtle move, Charlotte broke into a jog in order to catch up with Glen at the pigs-in-a-blanket platter. A few days before, Charlotte just happened to inadvertently mention to Glen that most of the town was saying Marlene was pregnant. "I would be careful if I were you. I bet Marlene is going to be chomping at the bit to find a man to help her raise that baby."

Charlotte knew this was the right thing to say in her efforts to divert Glen's attention away from Marlene. For, as much as Glen would like to have had a relationship with Marlene Prescott, the idea of adult responsibilities made him run in the other direction. A fling with a pregnant gal just didn't hold much appeal for Glen. Still, Glen couldn't help but notice that Marlene's figure seemed to be benefiting from her condition. Charlotte seethed as he pointed out, "I think her boobs look a little bigger than they did last week."

Charlotte responded, "Yeah, her boobs and her ankles. I think she's retaining fluid."

Chapter 11

Marlene, Allison, and Dorothy attended the Praise Alliance Church. It was a non-denominational church with a phenomenal preacher and an unbelievable choir that sounded like a band of angels. Marlene and Dorothy could neither one sing worth a lick, but Allison, her husband, and Tom all sang in the choir. Allison and Gary's kids usually sat with Marlene and Dorothy during the first half of the service. After the offering was taken, the kids went to Children's Church. Their daughter's chicken pox had spread to the son, so none of Allison's family was in attendance that morning. It was funny, but Marlene and Dorothy sort of missed having those squirmy little tykes sitting between them.

Marlene, Allison, and Dorothy all grew up in Praise Alliance Church. It's where they were all baptized. They'd shed tears on the altar, passed notes in the pews, been to countless covered dish suppers in the fellowship hall, got called down for giggling during a revival service and found out what's really important in this life. Allison and Dorothy got married in the sanctuary and Allison's kids were dedicated in front of the congregation. Sitting in a church doesn't make one a Christian anymore than standing in a milk barn will make one a cow; but being in those pews sure made Marlene, Dorothy, and Allison feel closer to God.

Tom and Dorothy met at church. Dorothy was on the membership committee when he moved into town. It was quite unusual for a young man to move to Coleman from somewhere else, seeing as the town didn't provide a whole lot of opportunity for most. Folks were much more apt to leave town than move to Coleman. Tom's first job after graduating college was as the director of Coleman Parks and Recreation. It was a job that Tom liked, but it wasn't his true passion.

When the town's budget was tight, Tom took it upon himself to take photos of Coleman's Parks and Recreation facilities. He then hung them all over town as a promotions campaign. The photos were so good that a local tourism board bought some to use for a brochure. Tom enjoyed doing the photographs so much that he quit his job with Parks and Recreation as soon as he saved enough start up money for his photography business.

When Tom first got to town, he was sought after by many a young lady who was intrigued by a young bachelor from Spartanburg, South Carolina. Thank goodness Dorothy was the one who got him!

On his first Sunday of living in Coleman, he visited the church. Tom was raised in a strict church-going home and said that when Sunday morning rolled around, even though he was in a new town and knew no one, he just couldn't imagine not attending church. "I started to sleep late and skip church, but then I thought about my mom. She used to call me every Sunday afternoon. I knew her first question would be whether I'd gone to church that morning."

So, Tom got up, put on his Sunday best and started walking. At that time, he was renting an apartment downtown, above the barber shop. He said he heard the most wonderful choir a few blocks away. He kept walking in the direction of the music to find a choir warming up a cappella on the front lawn.

The Sunday morning outdoor choir rehearsals brought more people into the church than any other outreach ministry.

Whenever the weather allowed, the choir met out on the lawn an hour before the service. They broke into sweet song that drew people in from miles around. Even people who lived near the church, but attended other places of worship said that the music put them in the right frame of mind while they were getting dressed and ready for church. If one person in town decided to protest, the Sunday morning outdoor choir rehearsals would have ceased.

One time, a woman who lived in the northeastern part of the state was visiting quaint little Coleman. The woman just happened to be an outspoken atheist who went around filing lawsuits against anything she felt violated her right to practice her non-beliefs. She and her husband were on their way to some courthouse in Tennessee that dared to display the Ten Commandments. Her plan was to stage a protest on the courthouse steps, demanding that the Ten Commandments be taken down.

Since she and her husband could not check into their hotel room in Tennessee until late afternoon, they decided to take a little detour which took them straight through Coleman. One could only imagine how offensive a Sunday drive through the town could be to one whose sensibilities were peaked at the very mention of anything related to faith or religion. It was difficult to find any businesses that were open on the Sabbath. Those that were didn't open until after noon and closed by six to allow employees to attend church. Typically, these merchants had signs offering discounts or free coffee to those who brought church bulletins. All over town were signs and banners displaying Biblical teachings and promoting prayer.

By the time our non-believing visitor had gotten through town, her intolerant nerves were raw. The final straw was hearing the choir on the front lawn. Her husband was ordered to drive to the church, where he parked the car. She got out and raised this big old ugly ruckus. Well, the choir director plainly told her that it was her right to file a complaint if she so wished, but until she went through the proper channels, the choir would continue to sing.

A choir member, who was also an off duty police officer, made a call to the station to give them a heads-up that the lady was probably coming down. She went into the station ranting and raving about the "repressed little armpit of a town" and ordered that the officers quickly take care of her because she had to be in Tennessee by two.

Then, a miracle occurred. Divine intervention intervened. The power went out, not all over town, just at the police station. Suddenly, Coleman's finest, typically professional and efficient, became a bumbling band of Barney Fife's. The station was pitch black and the computers were down.

The officers took just as long as they could to turn on flashlights, light candles, and find paper copies of forms that were usually done on the computer. Finally, the atheist lady left in a huff, uttering profanities that surely offended the man whom she didn't believe existed. She had bigger fish to fry in Tennessee and couldn't let Coleman's "incompetent, ill-prepared" police force hold her up.

That was the closest the choir ever came to having a formal complaint. Miss Atheist would have been so dismayed if she had known that her name appeared on the prayer request list each and every week.

Dorothy just happened to be on the membership committee when Tom decided to join the church. As tradition dictated, the committee met with Tom, explained the membership process and answered any of his questions. During that meeting, Dorothy was impressed with Tom's intelligence, commitment to his faith, and integrity as a human being. Tom and Dorothy soon struck up a friendship that grew into love.

Fellow parishioners rejoiced when Dorothy and Tom became husband and wife. They also showed compassion and prayed for the couple as they experienced the disappointment and frustration of infertility and trying to adopt. What a celebration they would have when Dorothy and Tom would bring their own little boy or girl to church for the first time!

Alas, even the most holy and sacred places could not be a total respite from The Hens. A few were members of the congregation and sadly, they sometimes dragged their evil ways right through the church doors. Whether it was whispering about what someone else was wearing or questioning another parishioner's salvation or both ("If she were truly a Christian, she wouldn't be wearing THAT!") The Hens couldn't keep their mouths shut, even in the house of the Lord.

During announcements, Francine, DeeDee's mom, asked that DeeDee's name be added to the prayer request list. DeeDee had some preterm labor symptoms on Wednesday and has been put on bed rest for the remainder of her pregnancy. Then, Francine started talking about DeeDee's cervix, which was a little more information than anyone needed to hear. Richard May, who stood at the podium during announcements and prayer requests turned beet red during Francine's description of her daughter's gynecological state of affairs.

Francine wound up in front of Marlene and Dorothy as they walked out of church after the service. Marlene asked about DeeDee. Francine told her that the doctors thought everything would be fine as long as she stayed off her feet. Then she added, "You know Marlene, the way you're on your feet all day at the pie shop can't be good for you."

Marlene and Dorothy both thought it was a strange comment, but Francine had always been a little odd. Marlene and Dorothy decided it best not to desecrate the Sabbath or the steps of a holy sanctuary by dwelling on bad thoughts about Francine or any of The Hens.

Chapter 12

Marlene and Dorothy were meeting at Bobby's for lunch. Allison couldn't join them, because both of her kids were still sick. This was the first time Dorothy could ever remember Marlene leaving Cutie Pies for lunch. Usually, she grazed on a salad or sandwich brought from home in between answering the phone, baking and waiting on customers.

"Dorothy, hiring Charity is the best business decision that I have ever made! It's so nice to be able to leave that shop and know that she can run things for me! You know how much I love running my business, but life can't be all about work. I'm planning on going to see Mom and Dad soon. I think Charity will be ready to take care of things."

Marlene's parents had officially become beach bums. They bought a place in Florida after her dad retired. She only got to go see them once or twice a year. In the past, she had to close the shop in order to go out of town. That's one of the main reasons she hired Charity, so that she could spend more time in Florida.

She also was hoping to gradually hire a few more people when she thought that Cutie Pies would be expanding. Marlene was definitely disappointed that the building beside her had been sold. Still, she just had a good feeling that she might be able to somehow get ahold of that space if she could just find out who the new owner was.

The sale of the farm would be finalized in a couple of days. Marlene was taking her parents their part of the money. It was enough to afford a lifestyle for them that they never enjoyed when they were younger. Marlene's grandparents had worked hard so that their kids and grandchildren could have a better life. Marlene felt a peace about selling the land, because, ultimately, the land would provide for them a life that her grandparents could only dream of.

Marlene had checked on having the old farm house moved to a new location and restored. She thought that part of her share of the money could be used for that, since her original plans for the money didn't pan out. Marlene hired a structural engineer from Roanoke to assess the old home. He determined that it was too old and in too much disrepair to survive such a process.

That afternoon, Tom was going over to the farm to take some photographs of the place. Marlene planned to make her parents a scrapbook so that they would always have the photos. More important than the photos were their memories of that old place. Marlene's grandparents were extraordinary. Their home was a place where everyone felt safe and comfortable. The land and the house were immaculately maintained not out of a sense of duty, but from the gratitude they felt to have land to work and a roof over their heads. Marlene was feeling a little blue over the sale. Going to Florida and seeing how happy and carefree her parents were down there would be reassuring.

Trips to Florida always inspired great pies. Whenever Marlene had been down there, she got the yearning to experiment with all sorts of tropical fruits. Two years ago, she came back from Florida and concocted a frozen pineapple slush pie with a coconut macaroon crust. It was like eating a big pina colada that could be shared with children and adults who didn't do libation. The year before, Marlene's Florida vacation gave birth to Dorothy's favorite pie of all times.

Marlene's parents had a tree just six paces from their kitchen door that produced the giant pink grapefruit. Marlene always brought back some of them to share with friends in Coleman. Every morning when she was in Florida, Marlene went out and picked one of the grapefruit, cut it in half, sprinkled brown sugar on it, and put it under the broiler. Under the heat of the broiler, the brown sugar and grapefruit juice caramelized. The pie she came up with was grapefruit custard filling with a broiled brown sugar topping. It was a beautiful pie, bright pink, with a golden, shimmering, crackly sugar glaze over the top. The taste was like a citrus crème brulee. Marlene thought it was great fun to make because she got to use a mini blow torch to melt the brown sugar over top of the pie.

Besides her parents and their grapefruit tree, there was one other thing that drew Marlene to balmy Florida. Mark was the realtor from whom her parents bought their Florida home. Marlene met him ten years ago when her parents first moved. She felt an instant spark when she met this man she described as exceptionally handsome. Dorothy and Allison had seen his picture and had to agree, he was gorgeous to look at!

He was tall with big hazel eyes and thick jet black hair sprinkled with just enough gray to make him look distinguished. Marks' grandmother was Cuban. From her he got gorgeous olive skin that tanned to a deep brown. Marlene had a thing for Latin men ever since she developed a crush on Erik Estrada when he was on "Chips."

Although the hazel eyes, great hair and olive skin made Marlene stop and take notice, she said it was Mark's smile that really grabbed her attention. Besides having perfectly straight teeth that were so white they gleamed, there was just a kindness and easiness about his smile that made him look approachable.

Mark felt the spark too. After the sale was finalized, he invited Marlene and her parents to have dinner with him. He said it was to celebrate the purchase of their new home; but really, he just wanted to spend more time with Marlene. She discovered that he was not only easy on the eyes, but also intelligent, funny, successful, and kind.

He'd never been married for much the same reasons as Marlene. Mark had been really busy in his career and also had very high standards for whom he would date. Marlene was the woman he said exceeded all of his standards and expectations.

Whenever Marlene was in Florida, they spent a great deal of time together. During the long interim between visits, the two talked on the phone, sent e-mails and just had a really nice courtship. They'd gotten to know each other pretty well and were ready to commit to something more serious. If Mark lived closer, the two would probably have been married.

The special at Bobby's that day was a sesame encrusted tuna steak on a bed of spicy noodles with a side of steamed asparagus and wasabi sauce. That was rather exotic fare for Bobby's. Fresh seafood was pretty hard to come by in little landlocked Coleman, with no interstate or airport for thirty-eight miles. The acquisition of fresh tuna steaks was quite a feat. Bobby's wife, Bea stopped by to chat and told them how they scored the case of tuna.

Turns out, one restaurant's misfortune had become their gain. Bobby's brother lived in a town about fifty miles southeast of Coleman where he ran a wrecker service. He was called out to tow a truck that had pulled over in the emergency lane of the interstate due to mechanical problems. The truck was bound for Knoxville, Tennessee with a load of seafood.

Bobby's brother also happened to be a pretty good mechanic. He checked the truck out before he attached the tow hooks, just to see if there were some way to get it started. What he found was a whole lot of problems that would take several hours to fix.

The discouraged truck driver put in a call to his boss and to the restaurant that was awaiting the delivery. His boss had no other trucks in the area that could be dispatched to take his cargo on to Knoxville. The restaurant he was taking the fish to prided itself on only serving seafood that was delivered fresh on a daily basis. If he could not get the seafood there within the next three hours, they would have to get fish to be served that night from another vendor.

Bobby's brother overheard the conversations between the driver, his boss and the restaurant in Knoxville. "How much would a man have to pay for your whole load of seafood?" Bobby's brother asked.

The driver was willing to sell it at cost. Otherwise, he was going to lose a whole shipment of fish. The ice in which it was packed was quickly beginning to melt.

Bobby got there within ninety minutes, loaded down with coolers and bags of ice. Monday, it was sesame encrusted tuna steak, Tuesday would be fried shrimp and Wednesday, a seafood buffet with anything that was left. Bobby's may not have promised that the seafood was delivered fresh that day, but it was the freshest seafood in Coleman!

Bea made the main dish herself. She once saw a chef on the cooking channel making sesame encrusted tuna and had always wanted to make it. Her first try turned out well. It was certainly the best tuna in Coleman. Dorothy and Marlene promised Bea that they would be back to try the seafood buffet. Before Bea went to check with the customers at the next table, she asked if they'd heard what other people had said about how they obtained the seafood. "Some of the Canasta Club ladies have been saying that we bought stolen seafood off a truck that was hijacked when it pulled off the interstate to get gas. One man who came in earlier said his wife refused to come with him because she thinks it's wrong to partake of food that was obtained by illegal means! I don't know how the story got so misconstrued!"

We all knew why it got misconstrued. The original story wasn't juicy enough because it didn't disparage anyone's character.

As Marlene gushed about Mark over her tuna, Jan and Millie walked by as they were being shown to their table. At least two Canasta Club ladies were not opposed to eating stolen fish. Of course, Jan and Millie were convicts after the colon bust! Jan leaned in towards Marlene and informed her that, "Some tuna contains harmful amounts of mercury."

She had some nerve to butt in like that after Allison put her in her place at the wedding! Marlene looked at Dorothy with a puzzled expression and asked, "What is the deal with their concern over what I'm consuming?"

Chapter 13

A sweet, lovable geek, that's what Allison's husband was in high school. Gary was short, skinny and uncoordinated. "A late bloomer" is how he described himself. Still, Allison, the pretty and popular cheerleader always loved to hang out with him. He made her laugh and would listen for hours as she told him goofy stuff about herself that nobody else in the world knew.

Secretly, Gary loved her for all those years, but kept his feelings between himself and his mom. When Allison's college boyfriend dumped her two weeks before the Senior Prom, she and Gary decided to go as friends. While Gary had dreams of making Allison fall in love with him that night, Allison was just happy to have a date with whom she felt comfortable and enjoyed being around.

At the end of the night, Gary got a sweet peck on the cheek and a hug rather than the passionate embrace he had imagined. Still, he had gotten to attend the Senior Prom with his dream girl and had the picture to prove it. That infamous prom photo still hung prominently over a table in Gary and Allison's foyer. Gary had a look on his face that could only be described as that of a fisherman who'd caught one for the *Guinness Book of World Records*.

After graduation, Allison attended college at East Tennessee State University and Gary accepted an academic scholarship at

Old Dominion. Something happened to Gary while he was in college. He grew taller, stronger and more confident. Gone was that awkward teenager and in his place was an extremely attractive man. Everything awkward about him went away and every good quality only got better.

Allison and Gary lost touch for a couple of years. She was dating a boy on the college baseball team from Mississippi. Although Gary was suddenly in the position of having girls fawn over him, he never got serious with anyone at Old Dominion. Always in the back of his mind was Allison. Allison, on the other hand became very smitten with her fast-pitching, slow-talking, hard-partying, good-time-boy from Dixie. She was smitten, that is, till he broke her heart.

It was Christmas Break of their junior year. Allison and her baseball stud had plans to spend some time in their respective hometowns with their families, and then meet in Atlanta to celebrate New Year's Eve together. He'd promised Allison a fancy dinner and dancing at a swanky Atlanta country club. His college roommate was a member of the club and his family had bought several tickets to the New Year's Eve Gala.

Allison's mom used to sew until she came down with carpal tunnel syndrome in her right hand. As soon as Allison came home for Christmas Break they began working on the most beautiful dress for Allison to wear for the gala. It was periwinkle with an empire waist, delicate spaghetti straps, and tiny sliver beads sprinkled all over it like little stars. Allison and her mom worked day and night to get that dress done before New Year's Eve.

Allison invited Dorothy and Marlene over to see the dress on the day before New Year's Eve. She decided to do a whole trial run of her holiday ensemble just so she'd look perfect on her special night. Her blond hair was piled on her head in a sleek up do, set off by a rhinestone hair comb. With her hair up Allison's grandmother's sparkly diamond earrings were displayed to perfection. Red lipstick, fluttery false lashes, that to-die-for dress, matching Peau de Soie pumps; Allison looked like a glamorous blond bombshell of a movie star!

Then, she got the call! Baseball jerk phoned while Marlene and Dorothy were at Allison's house. One day before their planned New Year's Eve celebration, he broke up with her over the phone! While he was home on Christmas Break, he and his high school sweetheart became reacquainted. His reasoning for handling the breakup as he did was that he thought it would give Allison a couple of weeks to mend her broken heart before they went back to school for Spring semester.

A couple of weeks! Allison's heart was shattered into a million pieces. This breakup would require a good few months to move through all the feelings of anger, pain, betrayal, and humiliation.

Allison was a mess when she hung up that phone! There she sat, on her bedroom floor, in that beautiful dress, crying and screaming up a storm! It was a heart-wrenching scene right out of a movie, except it was real, and her best friends had to witness it! Dorothy wanted to call that guy and tell him to go jump in the Mississippi River! Dorothy figured he must have been close to the Mississippi River, since he was in Mississippi and all. Dorothy was serious about giving that dumb, insensitive jock a piece of her mind, but Allison refused to give her his number.

If Dorothy couldn't tell that guy off, she had to do something to help her friend. Quickly, Dorothy and Marlene came up with a plan to get Allison out of the house for New Year's Eve. There would be no crueler irony than for her to spend New Year's Eve by herself, wearing her p.j.'s, instead of dancing in that gorgeous frock of which she and her mom were so proud.

Marlene and Dorothy were flexible with their New Year's Eve plans. By that time, Marlene had her first apartment. Their plans for the evening consisted of driving over to Langrid for some Chinese takeout, then going back to Marlene's apartment to watch Dick Clark drop the ball in Times Square.

Dorothy recalled that the National Guard Armory in Langrid was having a New Year's Eve dance. It wasn't exactly a country club gala. Still, it would be something to do and Allison could wear her dress.

Since Marlene and Dorothy had not planned on having an occasion to attend, they resorted to donning high school prom dresses. Dorothy's was about a size too small, thanks to the weight she'd gained post high school. They both looked and felt silly, but were driven by a higher cause. Allison needed some cheering up. Even if she was too upset to have a good time, at least she wasn't home by herself while that jerk from the Delta lived it up with his recycled high school girlfriend.

The party at the armory wasn't a real hip affair. Although there were people of all ages, most were of a fairly geriatric generation. Still, the girls had fun dancing to everything from swing music to that good party standard, "Celebration" by Kool and the Gang.

When slow songs would play, the three awkwardly and quickly exited the dance floor and hid inconspicuously in the corner. Those in attendance were nice enough people, but the gals weren't interested in any cheek-to-cheek swaying with any of them. Besides, this was a night for the girls!

Just as they had made themselves comfortable in the metal folding chairs they had claimed in the far east corner of the room, a rather handsome young man entered. He was impeccably dressed in a black suit, light blue shirt with a white pin stripe, and red silk tie.

Well, so much for girls' night. As soon as he walked in, each of them began scheming on how she would be the one to catch his eye first. Then, Marlene stepped up and declared what needed to be done. "Allison is the one who needs cheering up tonight. She gets first dibs on him. She needs to have a good story about dancing all night with a handsome stranger. Allison needs to have something good to tell that jerk if they run into each other at school."

Apparently, Marlene and Dorothy didn't need to get out of Allison's limelight in order for the mystery man to pick her over them. As they were talking, he'd made his way over to where they sat. "Hey, Allison, I haven't seen you in ages."

The voice was familiar, only deeper than any of them remembered. And he looked nothing like they remembered.

"Gary, I can't believe it's you!"

Allison sprung to her feet and gave him an embrace and a kiss on the cheek; kind of like prom night, but not really. This time, the intensity of Allison's attraction seemed to rival his.

Just then, an attractive older lady came up beside Gary and slid her arm through his. "Girls, this is my grandma. I've accepted the honor of taking her out this New Year's Eve."

How sweet was that? His grandmother had recently become a widow. Gary later explained that his grandfather had always taken his grandma to the dance on New Year's Eve. They were attending together to honor his grandfather's memory.

As if Allison didn't realize it, Marlene pointed out the obvious. "That guy's a class act if I've ever seen one!"

They watched in admiration as the geek who'd blossomed into an Adonis swung his grandmother around the dance floor. She laughed like a young girl, perhaps remembering all the happy times she had shared with her husband at the annual event.

When Gary's grandmother needed to take a breather, he fetched her some punch, then made a bee line for Allison. The two caught up and shared a few dances and memories of high school for the next half-hour or so, until Gary realized that his grandmother had fallen asleep while sitting by herself.

Allison, still brokenhearted, wasn't ready for another relationship, but definitely couldn't ignore her attraction to this boy whom she'd dismissed as friend-only material just a couple of years ago. Now, she had him on the back burner. When she was healed and ready to date again, Gary would be the one.

71

Gary and Allison returned to their respective campuses for spring semester, keeping in touch through letters and phone calls. Those letters and calls became increasingly more frequent as the semester went on and Allison's heart healed.

Allison knew she was ready for a new relationship when, right before she was supposed to come home for summer break, the baseball jerk stopped by her dorm room with a dozen roses. He said breaking up with her was a big mistake and that he'd do anything to get her back. This smooth talker said he'd even spend the summer with his aunt and uncle who were only an hour outside of Coleman just so they could spend time together over break.

Allison told him, "There's someone else," and meant it!

All she could think about was seeing Gary again. He'd be home for the summer, too; and she planned to make her feelings known!

Gary got home for summer break a few days after Allison. She planned to surprise him by being at his house when he pulled in the driveway. Allison was the one who got a surprise!

On the day that Gary was expected home, Allison called Gary's roommate, to find out what time he'd left. Allison remembered Gary saying that his roommate would be staying on campus all summer to do work on a research project with some of his professors.

Luckily, when she called, Gary's roommate answered. He informed her that Gary had been gone for about an hour. Allison carefully calculated the time she thought Gary would be arriving and planted herself in his driveway thirty-minutes before that. Allison didn't have to worry about his parents wondering why she was there. They were staying in a cabin in the Smokey Mountains for the weekend.

Allison put on her prettiest, sexiest, black sundress, slid into on some strappy black sandals, fashioned her hair into long spiral curls and glossed her lips in cherry red that was as shiny as patent leather shoes. The amped up, glammed up Allison drove over to Gary's house, and sat in his driveway. When she saw his car pull onto his street, she got out and stood leaning on her car, with a big smile as if to say "I bet you weren't expecting me!"

Well, obviously he wasn't. Before Gary could even get out of his car, a shiny little silver sports car pulled in behind him. In it was a cute brunette with big green eyes and a high teased pony tail. Her license plate was from Kentucky. Allison thought that perhaps this girl was lost and she had pulled in the driveway to ask for directions.

Gary got out of his car first, and then motioned for the pony tailed girl to get out of her car. He gave Allison a big warm hug before dropping a bomb on her. "Allison, I'd like for you to meet my girlfriend, Kaley. She's leaving her car here and we're going to ride up to The Smokies to meet my parents."

Kaley extended her hand to Allison. "It's nice to meet you. Gary has told me so much about you. It's so cool that his high school dream girl has become one of his best friends."

Allison didn't know if Kaley meant her statement the way it sounded, but she took it that Kaley was trying to let her know that her status with Gary had changed. Allison wasn't his dream girl anymore, according to Kaley, but was now just a friend. "Maybe I'm just trying to find a reason not to like her." Allison later told Marlene and Dorothy. "In a way, she seems sweet and she's a right cute girl. That big bushy ponytail looks a little like something that should be hanging off the back of Seabiscuit, but she is really attractive otherwise."

Allison had to quickly come up with a lie to explain why she was standing in Gary's driveway. It was her one chance to salvage her dignity and she wound up blowing it! "I came by to return something."

Allison hadn't yet thought of what that something was going to be. She slid into the driver's seat of her car and madly began rummaging for something, anything she could use to play off her story. All she could come up with was a cassette tape. It was a mixed tape of songs that the cheerleaders used when Allison was in high school. "Oh, gosh, you know what, I thought this belonged to you, but now I remember. It's actually Kimberly Lane's."

Allison elaborated to make her story sound more believable, all the while digging a deeper hole for herself. "I'm so stupid! I've been thinking all this time that this was a tape I'd borrowed from you our senior year, but the label clearly says it's a cheer mix tape. Sorry I bothered you. Nice to meet you Kaley!"

Allison drove off, embarrassed, humiliated, and broken-hearted. To make matters worse, when she checked herself in the rearview mirror, red lip gloss was all over her front teeth. That was the beginning of the summer that Allison lost her spunk and sunk into a funk. Her pride was so injured that she wouldn't even tell Marlene and Dorothy about the driveway incident until two weeks after it happened. The normally cute and perky Allison took to wearing no make-up, gaining five pounds and pretty much cutting off social interactions. Like a cola left out too long, her effervescence went flat.

The only time she got out of her house was to go to her summer job, babysitting the kids who lived two houses down from her. She functioned well enough to care for the kids without causing any physical or psychological damage. While she was babysitting, she'd muster up just enough energy to be pleasant, playful, and nurturing.

After the kids' mom would get home from work, Allison would walk home, eat dinner and then go into her room with a bowl of ice cream and a bag of chips. There she'd stay until the next morning. They knew things were bad when Allison's roots began showing. She was meticulous about having the highlights in her hair touched up every month. The owner of Curly-Q's even called to see if Allison was okay.

With the five pound weight gain approaching ten and six weeks of visible roots, Allison's mom was convinced that she had begun smoking pot. Allison's Uncle Ray had been a big pot head in the seventies. Allison's mom recalled him sitting in his room all the time, munching on junk food, and basically becoming a big slob who did nothing but suck oxygen out of the atmosphere. Just to get her mom off her back, Allison gradually began to snap out of it. She'd make herself put on make-up and got out of the house a little more. The extra weight came off quickly; she got her hair done and people began to see glimpses of the former Allison.

Still, beneath the façade that everything was getting better, Marlene and Dorothy knew that it would take quite a bit of time to heal her wounds, time and an unexpected phone call.

* * *

After the driveway incident, Allison avoided being anywhere she thought she might run into Gary. She was not only embarrassed; in all of the correspondence they'd exchanged during spring semester, not once did Gary mention having a girlfriend. Allison felt betrayed. There had been absolutely no contact between the two of them since that day, until one Saturday morning in July when Gary phoned Allison.

"Hey, Allison, it's Gary."

A dumbfounded Allison replied, "Hey, stranger."

She was surprised at how sarcastic she sounded. "Listen, I'm really sorry I haven't called this summer. I just had to take some time to think about things. We really need to talk. Can we go have lunch? I really need to discuss some things with you."

Allison's curiosity would kill her for the next few hours, but she knew it was best if she didn't pressure Gary to go ahead and spill it. Obviously, it was important for him to say whatever he wanted to in person. It was going to either be really good or really bad!

Allison decided to go casual in a pair of denim shorts, a red and white checked sleeveless top that tied at the waist and a pair of brown leather sandals. She pulled her hair back into a low ponytail and adorned it with a red grosgrain ribbon. Her reflection reminded her of Mary Ann from "Gilligan's Island." Allison recalled hearing about a survey in which men revealed that most preferred Mary Ann to Ginger if they had to choose between the two Gilligan cuties. She hoped that Gary would go for the Mary Ann look. The day in the driveway, when she had on the cleavage enhancing, slit to the thigh, black sundress, Allison was a Ginger. Maybe she'd do better as a Mary Ann!

Allison met Gary at twelve in front of Bobby's. Gary was wearing sunglasses, a t-shirt, khaki shorts, tennis shoes and a summer tan. As Allison approached him, he pulled her in towards him and gave her a tight hug. The hug was familiar, but a little better than all their previous hugs. Gary's arms and chest were toned from a summer of working on his uncle's dairy farm. She put her head on his shoulder, closed her eyes and drank in the woodsy smell of his cologne. Lunch and conversation seemed to only be a technicality at this point. Allison and Gary were finally in sync with their feelings for each other.

They realized their embrace was looking a little romantic when they heard a passerby on the sidewalk say, "Why don't they just get a room?"

Charlotte was the passerby. By that afternoon, the whole town knew that Gary and Allison were an item. Of course, Charlotte's story described them as "making out on the sidewalk in front of God and the world."

In the hours that lapsed between the embrace and everyone in town being alerted that there was a hot new romance, Gary and Allison had a lovely lunch of chicken salad sandwiches on toasted wheat. During their lunch, Allison learned that Gary had broken up with Kaley the week after the driveway incident and was ready for a new relationship.

As for the reason he hadn't told her he had a girlfriend, he didn't realize Allison liked him in that way until he saw her devastated look that afternoon she pulled out of his driveway. After lunch, they took a hand-held stroll through the park and shared their first kiss under the oldest tree in Coleman (at least that what the plaque on the tree said).

They were inseparable for the remainder of that summer. They managed to see each other every three weeks during their senior years of college and spoke on the phone nearly every night. The summer after they graduated college, Gary proposed; and they were married the next summer. It was a small but beautiful ceremony with Marlene and Dorothy sharing Maid-of-Honor duties.

Right after college, Gary landed a job in restaurant equipment sales. Marlene was his first and still one of his best customers. Marlene had a meeting with Gary set up for noon. It was part business and part personal. Marlene had been reading about the rich and famous serving fancy pies at weddings and other big events. Pie tins, while functional, were not particularly pleasing to the eye. The problem Marlene encountered was that her pies were almost impossible to transfer from the vessel in which they'd been baked. Marlene tried it a few times and the pies always fell apart. She needed some nice pieces that would work for both baking and serving. She was going to see if Gary could get her some things that would withstand high baking temperatures, but still look beautiful enough for a wedding. Marlene was determined to be a trailblazer. She would find a way to be the first in the area to market special occasion pies.

Gary was planning a great big surprise birthday party for Allison. He enlisted the help of Marlene and Dorothy. He had been taking great pains to set up secret meetings. It was of utmost importance that they kept their plans from Allison and from The Hens. Gary wanted Marlene's opinion on some of the ideas he'd come up with for the party. Since they were Meeting at Cutie Pies during the noon hour, Gary stopped and picked up two cheeseburgers, two orders of fries and a jug of sweet tea from Sally's Drive Inn.

As they dug into their burgers and fries, Marlene showed Gary a photo in one of her magazines of a pie display at a celebrity wedding in California. The center pie was about four times larger than the average pie. It was cut into squares rather than traditional slices and encircled by smaller pies that were on a lazy Susan sort of contraption. Gary promised to check with suppliers to find some similar pieces for Marlene. He had extra incentive to find those serving pieces. Gary thought that pies would be a great thing to serve for Allison's birthday.

Ingrid was shopping in the antique shop across the street from Cutie Pies. She was looking for curio cabinets to house her collection of gnomes. Ingrid had what was estimated by gnome aficionados to be one of the most extensive collections of gnomes in the Eastern United States. She was quite proud of her collection as it had led to sort of a celebrity status among fellow gnome collectors. A week before, her grandson Lucas broke five of her gnomes. Reportedly, only ten gnomes stood between her and someone else having the best collection in the Eastern U.S. Drastic measures were called for if Ingrid were to remain owner of the East's biggest gnome collection. She had gnomes in all sizes and engaging in all types of activities; from lounging on mushrooms to holding butterflies.

All of the garden gnomes had been moved indoors, including one that Ingrid described as "life size." Nobody wanted to argue with Ingrid, but it seemed the giant gnome wasn't authentically "life size" as far as gnomes go. It was more like human size, standing over five feet. Maybe there really wasn't such a thing as "life size" as far as gnomes were concerned since they didn't exist in the first place. By definition, they were mythical and imaginary as well as tiny and elfin. Ingrid's five foot gnome was creepy and not at all elf-like.

Ingrid hoped that locking up the curios would ensure that her remaining collection would suffer no harm. As she shopped, she talked to Patsy on her cell phone. "Gary's been in there for over an hour. He didn't have any restaurant supplies or catalogs with him today, just a big bag from Sally's. Those two are having lunch and Lord knows what else while poor Allison's home taking care of his kids!"

Chapter 14

Once a year, Allison took her engagement ring and wedding band over to a to a jewelry store in Langrid to have it cleaned and to have the prongs inspected. Allison's mom lost the diamond in her ring because of a broken prong. She had been out in their yard pruning rose bushes. Allison's mom always had the most exquisite rose garden. She cultivated more than thirty varieties of roses. Everything from traditional red and pink to a bush with flowers such a deep purple that they were almost black grew in her garden.

When she got back into the house, she took off her ring so that she could wash her hands and begin fixing dinner. As she reached down to remove the ring, she noticed that the stone was not in the setting. The woman crawled around that yard on her hands and knees for a month looking for that thing. She never did find it.

Allison's dad came up with what he felt was a plausible scenario. He thought that the sun made the diamond glisten, which attracted a bird, that carried it off and put it in its nest. As improbable as this explanation was, Allison said her mom even pulled a few birds' nests out of trees and tore them apart. Her dad allowed that it was pointless, considering that the diamond could have been picked up by a migrating bird that flew off to somewhere far away. Allison's mom hoped that the diamond at least wound up somewhere exotic, like Hawaii. Allison's mom always dreamed of going to Hawaii. The whole lost diamond ordeal made Allison exceptionally paranoid when it came to her ring.

Gary had to make sales calls to restaurants in Langrid, so he volunteered to take Allison's ring for its yearly prong check. What Allison didn't know was that the ring she would be getting back would not be the one she had sent with Gary. Part of her birthday surprise was going to be a dazzling bigger and better ring.

When Gary asked Allison to marry him, he slid a lovely half carat solitaire set in white gold on her hand. At their wedding, he presented her with a baguette studded band. Since that time, Gary had doubled the size of his sales territory and probably tripled the size of their income. Gary and Allison never would be so tacky as to discuss how much money he brought home; but Patsy McCrumb discussed it because Larry did their taxes.

That half carat that Gary gave her so many years ago was going to get a twin half carat solitaire. They were both going to be placed on either side of a two carat princess cut diamond. The baguette band was going to get an identical band and both would be welded to the ring, one on top and one on the bottom. The settings would all be changed to platinum. Gary planned to tell Allison that the jewelry store discovered a broken prong and had to keep her ring for a while in order to repair it.

Patsy ran to Sally's Drive Inn to pick up some food for the office. On her way there, she stopped by the dry cleaners. Allison was at the cleaners to pick up some of Gary's shirts. As she waited in line, Patsy was behind her and noticed that she was not wearing her ring anymore. When Patsy got into her car, she phoned Ingrid. "I saw Allison at the cleaners today. What I didn't see were her wedding rings! I bet she's found out about Gary and Marlene's little lunchtime rendezvous!"

Chapter 15

Allison's mom was having surgery, so Allison had to stay with her parents for the week. Gary was keeping the kids, but Marlene and Dorothy promised to help with them.

Allison and Gary had the cutest kids in the world! Cicilly was five. She had a head full of golden curls and full rosy cheeks. Since she was shorter than most kids her age, she looked more like a toddler than a school-aged child. Garrett was seven. He was also blond, but his hair was straight. Garrett idolized his uncle who was a Marine second lieutenant, so he kept his hair in a military-style buzz cut and saluted his parents whenever given a command.

Both kids were blessed with good looks, intelligence and sweet personalities. If Dorothy ever got to adopt, she wanted the child to spend lots of time around Cicilly and Garrettt in hopes that some of their good traits would rub off.

If one of Allison's parents were ailing, the other had to also. They, after all, did everything together. Allison's mom was having a hysterectomy, but somehow, her dad would develop symptoms. When Allison's dad had his hip replaced, all-of-a-sudden her mother diagnosed herself with arthritis in the hip. Allison thought that the other got jealous if one got too much attention.

Gary had been instructed to handle all household matters himself in that Allison would be in her own private little Hades.

Marlene and Dorothy were on standby in case any emergencies popped up.

Well, one day into managing the household, Gary encountered what he felt constituted an emergency. He was supposed to pick up Allison's ring that night and worried that he wouldn't be able to manage both kids in a shopping mall. Marlene and Dorothy were happy to assist. It was a good excuse to go shopping. Plus, Gary had promised to buy their dinner.

Charity joined in on their little outing. Her mama's birthday was coming up. Charity had to buy her present in time to mail it to West Virginia. When Joe came home they would be going to West Virginia to tell Charity's parents their good news. That would be the greatest gift of all. Charity said it was killing her not to be able to tell her mama!

They all went to the jewelers with Gary to pick up Allison's ring. It was absolutely breathtaking! All of the ladies took turns trying it on just for fun. Allison was going to be astounded when she found out that Gary was throwing her a lavish party and giving her an exquisite ring. She would feel like an absolute princess!

After the ring was placed in a fancy royal blue velvet box with robin's egg blue lining, Gary tucked it safely inside his front coat pocket. Then, they all decided to shop on their own for an hour and reconvene in the food court for dinner. Gary wanted to buy Allison some pretty lingerie in hopes that she would be exceedingly grateful for his efforts. There was just something a little twisted about Cicilly and Garrett helping Gary pick out sexy undies for their mommy, so Charity, Marlene, and Dorothy took the kids with them.

On their way to the toy store, Charity spied a new maternity clothing boutique. She went in while Marlene and Dorothy took the kids to look at toys. Charity wasn't showing yet, but would be within a matter of weeks. At her last appointment, the doctor told her that she needed to gain about five pounds over the month. Charity was so tiny that five pounds would really show on her. Cute little fitted tops and button-fly jeans would soon be replaced with roomy elasticized clothing.

Dorothy loved to be around pregnant women and felt honored to share in their joy; but, sometimes, she just couldn't help but be a little jealous. Dorothy wanted to shop for maternity clothes, have strange cravings and feel a tiny life grow inside of her. Over a dozen fertility specialists in four different states assured her that she would never be able to have a baby.

They all agreed that there was something terribly wrong with Dorothy's uterus. The last doctor described her womb as a "hostile environment for implantation." Some of the more kind doctors explained her malady with the utmost empathy and compassion. Others shrugged their shoulders and grew impatient with Dorothy's questions as they told her that she could never have what she'd dreamed of most all her life. Dorothy felt so cheated that something which happened so easily and naturally for most women could never happen to her. Sometimes she asked God, "Why?"

All she could figure was that there would someday be a child for whom she and Tom would be the perfect parents. When that happened, God would find a way to put that child in their home. They could not wait till that day!

Garrett and Cicilly talked Marlene and Dorothy into buying them a snow cone machine. It shaved ice and came with little paper cones and bottles of flavored syrup. Allison kept the most meticulous home. Hopefully, she would not wind up with a rainbow of bright snow cone syrup on her off-white sectional sofa. She was probably going to kill Marlene and Dorothy! In their defense, they both told the kids that the snow cone machine would have to be an outdoor toy. Easy for them to say when they were not the ones having to enforce that rule!

As the hour came to a close, they were all back in the food court. Cicilly and Garrett eagerly showed Gary their snow cone machine. They promised to make him a snow cone as soon as they got back home. Normally, Gary might have said no to such plans, but he was so desperate to keep his kids occupied that he'd probably let them dismantle his stereo system if that would keep them busy. Cicilly said that if she got really good at making snow cones she might open a snow cone store just like Marlene had a pie store. She was already naming off a list of flavors she planned to make and sell to kids in her neighborhood over the summer; grape, blue raspberry, mango, green apple, Cicilly had big plans for her and the snow cone machine. It sounded like Cicilly would give the ice cream man a run for his money!

Gary told Marlene and Dorothy about an interesting encounter he had while shopping for Allison's lingerie. As if he didn't feel awkward enough in the ladies underwear department or "panty-land" as he referred to it, Gary had to run into his great aunt Flossie. Flossie was really not blood relation to Gary, which he was very quick to point out. She was his grandmother's best friend and all the grandchildren wound up calling her "Great Aunt Flossie" for some reason. Gary was ten before anyone told him that Flossie wasn't really his great aunt. He met the news with great relief. Flossie was eccentric to put it mildly. Gary was glad to know that her craziness wasn't a genetic concern for him. With diabetes, club feet, crooked teeth, eczema and cellulite running in his family, Gary didn't need any other genetic anomalies to worry about. Fortunately, he and his children seemed to have extracted the best genes from his pool.

Gary couldn't help but notice, and be disgusted by, the fact that Flossie was looking at some fairly racy undies for a lady of her age. Gary had seen Flossie in her underwear and the memory forever haunted him. He was fourteen, and the whole family had gathered at his Grandma's house for Sunday dinner. After church, everyone changed into comfortable, forgiving, eating clothes. Gary decided to change in his grandmother's downstairs bathroom. The door was closed, but not locked.

Gary opened the door to find Flossie standing there in her skivvies.

It seems that those things we most want to forget will not repress themselves, but rather remain a vivid image in our mind's eye. A shudder still ran through Gary as he described Flossie's waist-high white panties with a tummy control panel and her over- the-shoulder-boulder-holder, industrial material tan bra. The outfit was made even more memorable by Flossie's knee-high orthopedic hose.

As bad as that image was, seeing Flossie hold a pair of black silk panties disturbed Gary even more. Seems Flossie had found her a man. She was getting married at the courthouse the next week and was buying some new underwear for her wedding night. "I figured I best get some new stuff. Why the panties I got on right now are held together with safety pins."

Way too much information!

Charity met the rest of the group carrying a bag full of maternity clothes. She announced that she was famished. That baby was ready for some food! Gary and Marlene sat and watched everyone's bags while the others got their food. Across from the food court, Annie Brooks, best friend of Jan's daughter, was working in the music store. She was on the phone with her mother. "Gary and Marlene are sitting in the food court together, just talking and laughing. I guess they think they won't see anyone they know in Langrid. Get this; she has a big bag from the maternity store!"

Annie's mom shared some news that she'd heard. "Well, I happen to know for a fact that Allison has moved out of their house and is staying with her parents!"

Chapter 16

It was the first day for the trial of "Carla the Illegal Colon Cleanser," It was a big deal in Coleman. In fact it had made international news. It was just one of those freaky, bizarre stories that interested people even though most wouldn't admit to it. Some citizens felt that it was degrading and made Coleman look foolish to the rest of the country, the "butt" of their jokes. Perhaps, but most found it hilarious that Millie and Jan were getting such broad exposure!

The Hens held a candlelight prayer vigil the night before in Jan's front yard. Millie and Jan were not facing criminal charges, but they did have to take the stand. The whole ordeal put them both in a brittle state. Mille had dropped ten pounds in the last month. "Poor thing looks so frail," is how Patsy described her.

It wasn't as though she were wasting away. She could have dropped twenty more pounds and still have been considered obese. Jan had been having anxiety attacks and episodes of crying. When the whole thing was over, people were betting that Millie and Jan would get after somebody for pain and suffering money!

Half the town got to the court house early in the morning to view the proceedings. A flock of Hens were holding signs outside of the courthouse that said, "We love you Jan and Millie!"

Dorothy thought about going down there with a sign saying, "I stand behind Jan and Millie," or "Jan and Millie, we've got your backs!"

Dorothy, Marlene and Allison would love to have been flies on the wall in that courthouse, but decided not to attend. They realized that court proceedings were a serious matter and are not meant for public entertainment. Still, their sinister halves were dying to be there! Marlene and Dorothy were meeting for lunch at one. Court recessed at noon, so they'd be able to find out something. If Allison escaped from her parents' house, she'd meet them too.

Allison's mom and dad were about to drive her up the wall! Her mom was having some discomfort and was all depressed because she didn't like the fact that the doctor took out her female parts. Allison's mom was sixty-something. It wasn't like she was going to have any more babies. The doctor said she may just have been suffering from hormonal fluctuations, and that could be treated. Since her dad never had ovaries, he couldn't complain of the exact same symptoms as her mom; but he did say that he was having pain in his nether regions. He allowed that he'd pulled his groin. The most physical activity he'd gotten since Allison had been there, was walking from the couch to the fridge. Perhaps he might have needed to stretch before doing that.

Dorothy got to Bobby's a little before one to get a table. It was packed with people from the courthouse. Fortunately most of them had finished their lunch and were heading back to court. Bobby's wife cleaned up a table for them and told Dorothy all the chatter she'd heard about the trial so far.

Carla, the Illegal Colon Cleanser, claimed to possess a degree in the healing arts from an online college. According to the judge, that did not qualify her to practice colon cleansing or make moonshine. Plus, her degree from the online institute was dated two weeks after her arrest. Millie took the stand right before lunch. She told of their visit to the seedy operation as if they thought they were going to a day spa. In a cruel turn of events, she had to implicate a fellow Hen who had recommended the cleaning service.

Jan was to take the stand after lunch. Jan had told several people that her recollection of the events from that day were blurry because of the moonshine elixir she was given.

Dorothy did know for a fact the woman couldn't handle her liquor. One time, Larry had a Christmas party at the office. Patsy invited all The Hens to it. Larry had bought some chocolate truffles filled with rum and put them in a candy dish. After eating three of them, Jan's husband had to take her home because she was so loopy.

Marlene came in wearing her new pair of stilettos. She had ducked into a shoe store at the mall while Dorothy was paying for Cicilly and Garrett's snow cone machine. The shoes were in the window, and she just had to have them. They were definitely not shoes to work in. Marlene had worn a pair of flats to work and changed into her high heels before going to lunch. When Marlene wore heels, they turned her into someone else. All of a sudden she carried herself like a runway model. With her hips pushed forward and shoulders pushed back, she sashayed into Bobby's. Marlene had drawn some attention of which she was totally unaware.

Louise Franklin, the most hateful woman in Coleman, gave Marlene a big dose of the evil eye as she passed her. Marlene plastered on a broad smile and, in her sweetest voice, commented to Louise that it was such a lovely day. Marlene always did that to Louise, and Louise just did not know how to handle pleasantries. Most would rather have crossed the Sahara Dessert in a blinding sandstorm than cross that shrew on her best day. Marlene, on the other hand loved to mess with her. Louise replied, "This is just the kind of weather that gets my allergies all messed up. It's nice that you can enjoy this weather, but it will put me in bed sick before this week is over!"

Marlene wished Louise a quick recovery from her impending allergy attack before taking a seat.

Allison called about five minutes after Marlene arrived to tell them she wouldn't be able to make it. Allison's dad heard that there was a bad stomach virus going around. He was afraid that if Allison got out, she would bring it in on him and her mother. She had two more days at her parents' house. If they got sick, it would only lengthen her stay in purgatory. She was not taking any chances!

Patsy's niece, Amy, was seated close to them. She leaned over to compliment Marlene on her shoes. Then she added, "You'd better be careful in those things. A fall wouldn't be good right now."

Marlene just rolled her eyes after Amy turned back around. "Hens have been saying the oddest things to me lately!"

Dorothy was surprised to find Patsy at the office when she returned from lunch. She expected her to be off every day until the court case was over. She was telling Larry that the judge halted proceeding for the rest of the day. It seemed Jan developed a migraine during lunch and was just not up to testifying. Patsy asked Dorothy how her lunch with Marlene was. Dorothy started to ask her how she knew who she had eaten lunch with, but The Hens seemed to know everything. They had an organized network; and they were planted all about town, spying on the unsuspecting.

"I heard Marlene was teetering around on four inch heels. She ought to know better than that!"

Chapter 17

Marlene, along with half the other people in Coleman caught the dreaded stomach virus. Fortunately, it only lasted about twenty-four hours. Unfortunately, it hit her at work. One minute she was waiting on a customer; the next, she was out behind the shop hurling. She called her doctor who told her to go home, rest and drink plenty of fluids. Charity was working, so Marlene left her in charge of things.

Allison, who was done taking care of her parents, was still in the nurse mode. She went over to help Charity. Marlene was afraid that Charity would catch the virus, which could be really bad for a pregnant woman. Allison instructed Charity to leave for about an hour while she bleached the counters and sprayed the place down with an antibacterial agent.

On the way out to her car, Marlene was overcome with nausea. It was bad enough that she had to puke in the landscaping behind her shop, but worse because Donna Tate's husband saw it happen. At dinner, Donna's husband told her about seeing Marlene getting sick that morning. After dinner, Donna called Leila. "Marlene is having some bad morning sickness. My husband saw it with his own eyes!"

Chapter 18

After she had recovered from her ailment, Marlene decided that it might just be a good time to visit Florida. Charity's husband wasn't going to be coming back for two more weeks. Charity had asked for Marlene to give her more hours until he got home. The anticipation of sharing her good news with him was about to drive her crazy. She thought having more to do until he got home could be a good thing. Marlene was, of course, excited about seeing her parents, but couldn't wait to see Mark. They'd been talking more frequently. Now that Charity was working for her, Marlene hoped they could see much more of each other.

Marlene would be taking her parents a very thoughtful and sentimental gift on this trip. After they decided to sell the farm, Marlene had Tom go down to the farm and take photographs. He spent the whole day there and shot some beautiful landscapes. It was a series that depicted scenes from what was a typical day for Marlene's grandparents.

The first photo was of the sun coming up. There were pictures of the farm house, the barns, fields, water troughs, and the silos. The final photo of the series was of the sun setting. Marlene had put the photos in a beautiful leather bound scrapbook. She had Dorothy do calligraphy captions with each photo. A pocket in the back of the scrapbook held recipes from her grandmother, receipts from the farmer's coop and pages her grandfather had torn from *The Farmer's Almanac*. She'd thought about mailing it, but wanted to be there when they opened it.

Since she was leaving the next morning, Marlene ran by Coleman Pharmacy to pick up some things for her trip. As the cashier rang up her sunscreen and travel sized toiletries, she asked if Marlene were going anywhere special. "Oh, I'm going to Florida to visit my parents."

As usual, the pharmacy was crawling with Hens. Louise was shopping for medication. Surprisingly, she was not in the section for allergy medications. It was pain relievers she was shopping for that day. Every change of weather brought on a different ailment. The chill that had fallen upon the evenings had made her arthritis act up.

Just to antagonize Louise, Marlene complimented her on the sweater she was wearing. Never being able to respond pleasantly to a compliment, Louise lamented, "I hate this sweater. It makes me itch; but I've got to wear it today; or I'd freeze to death!"

In the whole history of mankind, there probably had never been a person freeze to death in fifty-eight degree weather, but Marlene decided it best not to point that out. When she heard Marlene saying that she was going to Florida, Louise began verbally listing all the things she hated about the sunshine state: "Too hot, mosquitoes, foreigners, wild college kids on Spring Break and too many elderly people who drive slow." The list went on and on.

Marlene asked, "What part of Florida have you visited?"

Louise snapped, "Oh, I've never gone and never will. You couldn't pay me enough to go down there. I've never talked to anyone who's had good things to say about that place!"

Marlene felt a need to defend the state that had provided such a fun backdrop for her parents' retirement. "Well, you haven't talked to my parents, because they are in love with the place. You might like it down there, being so sensitive to the cold and all."

Louise snapped back, "I don't think so! My sister went down there for vacation last summer. She's still vacuuming sand out of her car. I hate sand. It gets everywhere."

There was obviously no convincing Louise that Florida was anything more than a cesspool.

DeeDee's mom, Francine, was talking to the pharmacist about some medicine DeeDee was taking to stop her preterm labor contractions. All the while, she was listening to Marlene. Francine delivered the prescription to DeeDee and shared some new findings. "I heard Marlene talking about going to Florida to see her parents. What do you want to bet she'll stay down there to have the baby?"

"Or," DeeDee added, "she may be going down there to have something done about her pregnancy."

Chapter 19

Dorothy had a lunch time appointment to get her hair done at Curly-Q's. She was obsessed with keeping her gray covered. She had a standing appointment every month to get her color done. Dorothy had a pact with her hairdresser, Clarissa Donavan. If Dorothy were ever in a coma on coloring day, Clarissa would come to the hospital and color her hair. In exchange, Dorothy had promised to wax Clarissa's upper lip and tweeze her eyebrows if she ever fell into such a state. Clarissa kept trying different cutting techniques on Dorothy's hair. Dorothy was convinced she'd one day find the style that would allow her to set those curls free on a daily basis!

The Colon Case was still all the talk. Dorothy figured that it would be the topic during her appointment. In a surprise twist, Carla the Colon Cleanser and her boyfriend, Bucky, the Bootleg Moonshine Runner testified against each other. It was part of a plea agreement. He testified about her cleansings and she told of how he produced and transported moonshine. In exchange for their testimonies, neither would serve any jail time. They both had community service to complete and were on strict probation. Some deputies went and dismantled Bucky's moonshine still.

That should have been where it ended, but this strange case had just gotten more bizarre. Deputies may have seized Bucky's still, but they didn't find the jars of moonshine he had buried in the woods behind their house.

Since the trial, Carla had seen herself as a martyr, willing to risk jail time, in order to wash dirty colons of those who needed the service. "I have a gift. I am a healer."

When she was arrested again, that was her statement. She didn't come up with this on her own. No, it came to her in a dream. Carla dreamed of a messenger telling her to continue in her illegal ways. The messenger said that she possessed special powers to make sick people well.

Next morning, Carla and Bucky loaded up their minivan with moonshine jars, and her colonics equipment. They rolled across the state line, a blatant violation of the terms of their probation. Their plan was to travel the country, performing illegal colonics under the influence of illegal beverages.

To Carla and Bucky's demise, they forgot to pack some snacks before embarking on their mission. A couple of hours into the pilgrimage, they got hungry and had to stop for breakfast. They went to a little pancake house where half the people in there were reading newspapers with Carla and Bucky's picture in them. Somebody from the diner called the police and so ended their journey.

Patsy was all to pieces, afraid that her friends would be drug through the court system when the new trial began. Patsy had been so distressed by the whole thing that she had to leave town for the weekend and go on a wild shopping spree. Larry was more than happy to oblige. She'd been getting on his last nerve!

When Dorothy showed up for her hair appointment, she was surprised to see that Rhonda, formerly of Leila's, was working at Curly-Q's. Turns out retirement didn't suit Carol Reece, so she was back styling hair and pumping customers for disreputable information. With Carol back to work, Rhonda was out of a job. Curly-Q's was looking to expand their clientele and needed another stylist. It was a move that seemed to suit Rhonda just fine. "That place was driving me nuts! I heard enough slander and lies about people to do me for a lifetime! And all the soap operas; those women acted like it was their own lives being played out on that little dinky TV."

Dorothy was itching to ask Rhonda details about what was said in Leila's, but decided against it. She didn't want to appear as catty as her previous patrons. Plus, Dorothy was not sure if she could trust Rhonda yet. That old saying goes, "If you lay with dogs, you'll wake up with fleas."

Even if Rhonda was of pure heart and intentions before working at Leila's, her time in that place may have planted some bad seeds.

Clarissa Donavan owned Curly-Q's. She was a former big city girl from Dallas, Texas, who married a Coleman farmer. Clarissa stood out in Coleman. Thanks to frequent trips back to Dallas, she had the latest styles before anyone else around Coleman. When folks heard a chick from Dallas was moving to Coleman, they were expecting a rodeo darling with big Texas hair, lots of makeup, flashy clothes, a ten gallon hat and belt buckles the size of a dinner plate. Clarissa defied that stereotype. Tall and svelte, she was usually dressed in simple, but well-made clothes. Her outfits were always perfectly accessorized with chunky necklaces, a wrist full of bangles, dangly earrings and good quality shoes. Clarissa hoped that the salon would eventually make enough money for her to open up a nice clothing and accessory boutique.

Clarissa also did Marlene and Allison's hair. As she trimmed and styled Dorothy, they caught up. "How are your counterparts?" she asked.

Dorothy told her about Allison's recent stay at her parents' house and about Marlene's trip to Florida. Since she was up on the latest trends, Dorothy also asked if she'd heard about people serving pies at fancy occasions. Clarissa had indeed read about the pie mania. If the clothing boutique came to fruition, she vowed to serve Marlene's trendy pies at the grand opening.

Rhonda then asked Dorothy how Marlene was holding up. Apparently, the girl did learn a thing or two about eavesdropping at her previous job. "She's doing great," Dorothy replied; "is there any reason she shouldn't be?"

"No, not really, it's just got to be hard going through that alone."

"Through what," Dorothy asked?

"Having a baby," replied Rhonda, stunned that Dorothy didn't know what she was talking about.

Dorothy's face burned hot with anger. The Hens had gone way too far! It all made sense; the comments made about Marlene drinking at Gretchen's wedding, eating tuna, wearing spiked heels.

Rhonda shared all the details, revealing a menacing and premeditated effort to take random details from Marlene's life in a desperate attempt to support their salacious assumptions. Dorothy's fury increased as she was informed that The Hens also tried to stain the reputation of her other best friend's husband by naming Gary as the father. Dorothy's first inclination was to call Marlene and Allison to organize their retribution, but she'd learned not to go with her first inclination when her mind was clouded with rage.

No, this would take some self-control. The Hens were impulsive and haphazard. Dorothy would beat them at their own game by being patient and calculating. Marlene, Allison, and Dorothy always made a great team. Dorothy would lay in wait until Marlene came back to town and they could all talk in person. After all, great schemes are not devised over the phone. Some high level strategic planning would go into settling the score. The Hens needed to watch out! They had met their match!

Chapter 20

The weather in Florida was glorious. The mornings were warm; the days weren't unbearably hot; and the nights were breezy and clear. It was the perfect paradise for Marlene to spend time with her parents and the man of her dreams.

Mark picked Marlene up at the airport. Marlene was always excited to see him; but this time, her stomach was doing flip-flops during the whole flight. She prayed that it was excitement and not residual symptoms from her stomach virus! There was something different about him this time. He had this mischievous twinkle in his eyes that Marlene had not seen before. Mark had never before been affectionate with Marlene in public, but this time he picked her up off the ground and planted a big kiss on her right in the middle of the airport. Marlene didn't know what had gotten into Mark, but she sure did like it.

She noticed that he seemed to have gotten even more handsome since the last time she'd seen him. He'd taken off from work that week. It wasn't often that Marlene had seen him so casually dressed. Instead of his usual suit and tie, he was wearing khaki shorts, a blue and white Hawaiian shirt and a pair of flip flops. It was pure Florida, Jimmy Buffet casual. His designer sunglasses were resting on top of his head. The weekend before, Mark and some friends had gone deep sea fishing. He still had a little bit of sunburn on his nose from that excursion. Mark was a few years older than Marlene, but still had a boy-like quality about him. Maybe it was his sheepish sly grin and those deep dimples. The only giveaways that he was approaching fifty were those little streaks of gray running through his hair.

Mark carried Marlene's luggage out to the car. She noticed how toned his forearms looked as he effortlessly tossed her fifty pound suitcase into his trunk. "You got a new car. When did you do that?"

Mark's little convertible sports car had been replaced by a sport utility vehicle, loaded with all the amenities. "I've wanted something I can haul my dog and my golf clubs in. Besides, I might need something to get up those steep, winding mountain roads up where you live."

"What? You've only come to Coleman one time, and that was when you were passing through on your way to Cincinnati."

"Well, Marlene, I've been thinking about cutting back on my work to make more time for us. I see this relationship going somewhere. I've got to see you more often."

If Mark cut back on his hours and Marlene kept Charity working in the shop, this long distance relationship might just have a shot!

Mark took Marlene to her parents' house. Merle and Glenda Prescott had fully immersed themselves in the Florida way of life. Marlene's father had taken to wearing Bermuda shorts, t-shirts, and sun visors, quite a change from the overalls and plaid flannel shirts he wore in Coleman. Her mom stayed all sun kissed and toned thanks to daily jogs along the beach and active involvement in a tennis league. She'd traded in her dowdy khakis and polo shirts for sundresses, Capri pants, and sandals that showed off hot pink painted toenails. Marlene loved seeing them enjoy this life for which they worked and saved so diligently. Both of them looked at least ten years younger than when they left Coleman.

Glenda had laid out a fabulous looking lunch. There was steamed shrimp, corn on the cob, roasted red potatoes and chocolate sheet cake for dessert. Marlene loved to see Mark with her parents. He fit right in with her family and had from the first day he met her folks. Mark and her dad often played golf together or went out to lunch. During lunch, it seemed like Mark and her parents had something going on that Marlene was not in on. Was he planning something that she didn't know about?

After lunch, Marlene presented the scrapbook to her parents. As she predicted, they became a little emotional, but in a good way. That farm had so many good memories that excavators and developers could never take away. They declared it the best gift she'd ever given them, and they thought that Tom's photos were masterpieces.

Chapter 21

Tom had not gone to work because he was the latest victim of the stomach flu that had ravaged the town. It was the worst possible timing. He was supposed to photograph an advertisement campaign for a local auto dealer. It was a beautiful day; the sky had provided perfect lighting for outdoor photographs; but he'd had to reschedule. Tom said there was no way the reschedule date would ever be as perfect for photographs. The particular car dealer for whom he was working didn't like advertisements showing cars in the showroom. He liked action photography, outside, with the car in motion.

To make matters worse, the car dealer had a beautiful model signed on for the campaign. The model happened to be his niece, who had done a great deal of work in fashion shows and commercials. She was in from California to visit family and agreed to shoot the campaign. It was the kind of thing that could have really advanced Tom's career. He hoped that he'd feel better that afternoon or at least by the next morning in that the model/niece would only be in town for two more days. Shooting this type of ad could lead to lots of more work for Tom. He made a nice living with weddings and studio appointments, but advertisements were where some real money could be made.

Dorothy was worried about leaving Tom at home by himself. He was so sick that she was afraid he might dehydrate. Tom convinced her to go on to work, which sort of relieved Dorothy. She was afraid of being around him and catching that dreadful illness. Besides, the very sound of someone throwing up made her want to do the same!

A few hours into her workday, Tom called. He was so frantic that Dorothy couldn't understand anything he was saying. She was convinced he was so ill that he'd begun talking out of his head. "I'm leaving now to come home and take you to the doctor."

Right as Dorothy was about to hang up, he summoned his voice. "No, no, it's not that. The adoption agency just called. We're getting a baby!"

Dorothy wanted to burst into tears of joy right at her desk, but Patsy was standing within three feet of her making coffee. Last time the couple thought they were getting a baby, it fell through at the last minute. Patsy went around saying that the adoption agency dropped them because they did a drop-in visit and the house wasn't clean. Truth is, the natural mother and father had gotten back together and decided to raise the baby. Dorothy didn't want Patsy to know what was going on until she was sure that they'd be getting a baby.

Tom explained that a young single mother in Tennessee had a three-month-old baby that she'd decided she didn't want to raise. There was no father listed on the birth certificate and no suitable next of kin to whom they could give the child. It was an emergency situation, meaning, they should be getting their baby really soon! Dorothy told Tom she loved him and couldn't wait to get home to celebrate. Patsy mumbled under her breath, "He must not be too sick if he feels like celebrating."

Chapter 22

On Marlene's last night in Florida, Mark told her that he had a special surprise. They would start the evening by going to dinner with Marlene's parents and the surprise would come later. As Marlene got ready, her mom fussed about what her daughter would wear. "Mom, it's just dinner, not a debutante ball."

"Yes, honey, but I just think that teal sundress looks so pretty on you. Don't you want to dress up for our last dinner of this trip? Wear something that will stick in Mark's mind after you leave."

Giving into her mother's wishes, Marlene changed out of her pink cotton skirt and sleeveless knit top into her teal dress and silver sandals. That week she'd bought a silver necklace with glass beads that matched the dress to perfection. Thanks to a few days of vacation, Marlene was tan and rested. Once the change was complete, Marlene had to agree with her mother, she did look darn good in the teal sundress.

Marlene rode to the restaurant with her parents. Mark went early to get them a table. When they arrived, Mark was the most handsome Marlene had ever seen him. He was wearing dark pants with a small pinstripe and a light blue dress shirt, casually undone to the third button, and the sleeves rolled up to the middle of his bronzed forearms. It was that Florida professional style that's sort of dressed up but still casual and carefree. He jumped up from his seat when he saw them walk in and kissed Marlene right there in front of her parents. It was a kiss that made her weak in the knees. He smelled as good as he looked; an intoxicating mixture of salty sea spray and warm cedar. Marlene wanted to fall into his arms right there in the restaurant, but maintained her composure. "Told you he'd like that dress," her mom whispered as they walked to their table.

Besides seeing her parents and Mark, Marlene's favorite thing about visiting Florida was eating at The Old Dock. As the name suggested, it was an old refurbished fishing dock. The building sat over the water on stilts, so that waves rolled right underneath. The space was small and intimate. It was furnished in a mismatched flea market style. Everything inside looked hand painted and weathered. The tables and chairs had a rich patina of crackled layers of paint in various colors. Glass containers filled with smooth jewel-toned sea glass, tumbled smooth by the ocean, lined shelves along the walls. Flickering candles on every table lent a warm romantic glow to the whole place. Diners looked luminous and serene, bathed in the soft candle glow. Hand dyed burlap placemats and drinks served from Mason jars gave it a rustic feel.

The story behind the restaurant and its owners was quite intriguing. "I sell seashells," is the first thing Gabrielle said when she met her husband, Brice.

When the native South Floridian surfer dude heard that sweet East Tennessee twang, he melted right there in his flip flops.

Gabrielle used to sell seashells; in fact, she sold tons of them. She used to ship them by the bushel to landlocked locations all over the world. To understand how this mountain girl wound up living on the seashore, making her living selling shells, one must go back to her childhood.

When Gabrielle was twelve, her family took a trip to Myrtle Beach, South Carolina, a Southeastern vacation spot, filled with amusement parks, putt-putt golf, and t-shirt shops. Its diverse array of attractions made it a popular spot for both families and high school seniors who had just graduated and wanted to celebrate their newfound freedom with a week of partying on the coast.

Until that time, the girl had only fantasized about the sand, the ocean and the shells. One whiff of that sea air and the little girl knew she'd found her calling. For five magnificent days, she rode waves in the ocean, buried her toes in the sand and combed the shore for shells. Her parents had to plead with Gabrielle to come in for dinner in the evenings. She would be up with the sun so that she would not miss a minute of beach time. When it came time to return home, she cried; and the sobbing was nearly nonstop for the eight hour drive home.

For the rest of her adolescence, Gabrielle was a conflicted soul. She was fond of her hometown in the mountains, but the ocean had a bizarre hold on her psyche. During high school, her bedroom was covered with shells and pictures of various beaches from around the world. Gabrielle spent a good deal of her time immersed in a fantasy world full of sand and sea mist.

After college, Gabrielle bade her family a tearful ado and made her home on Sanibel Island, Florida, one of the world's foremost seashell gathering spots. With little cash, but plenty of imagination, she launched her one woman company.

Shells on Sanibel were as plentiful as acorns in Gabrielle's native Tennessee mountains. Shells were free and they were plentiful. Gabrielle reasoned that selling them would be nearly one-hundred percent profit!

So, armed with a big dream and a bunch of shell baskets, Gabrielle woke with the sun and trekked to the beach every morning. With her tan skin, cutoff shorts, and blond ponytail, she looked much like that little girl who first fell in love with the beach. Gabrielle mastered the business of selling sea shells, pairing it down to a science: search, sanitize, sort, and sell.

After Gabrielle completed her daily shell search, she would return to her quaint little beach cottage where the shells were dumped into buckets of bleach. The bleach cleaned the shells and also got rid of any critters' remains. Next, the shells were sorted by category. Finally, the shells were shipped to all sorts of locales, to be used for everything from interior décor, to jewelry, to landscaping.

It was one morning while collecting shells that Gabrielle met up with Brice. Fresh out of culinary school, Brice had gotten a job at an upscale restaurant on the island. His workday began at noon when he'd prep ingredients for his nightly creations. The schedule allowed him to spend his mornings surfing.

For a couple of weeks, he had noticed this cute girl collecting shells. He came up with a scheme to get her attention. Brice usually didn't hit the surf until around nine every morning. Phase one of his plan was to figure out what time Gabrielle was going out to the beach.

On the first day of phase one, Brice was on the beach by eight thirty, only to find that Gabrielle was already there. Day two of phase one, Brice was on the beach at eight. Still, Gabrielle beat him. If this night owl was going to carry out his plan, some sleep would have to be sacrificed. On day three, Brice was on the beach at six in the morning, a tall order considering that he hadn't gotten off work until midnight the night before.

Alas, he was on the beach before the dreamy little blond sea urchin. Brice began on a quest to find the most beautiful, unique shell on the beach. After combing the shore for a few minutes, he spotted a large clam shell. Luckily, both the top and bottom of the shell were still connected. Inside, the shell was a pearlescent pink.

About thirty minutes after Brice's quest for the most perfect shell of the morning had begun, Gabrielle hit the beach. Brice ran up to meet her with his find. "Hey, I've noticed that you shell hunt every morning. I saw this and thought you might like it. What is it you do with all these shells anyway?"

That's when Gabrielle uttered the amazingly cute opening line of their story. "I sell seashells."

Immediately, Brice recalled an episode of "The Brady Bunch" when Cindy Brady recites the tongue twister, "She sells seashells by the seashore," in an attempt to lose her lisp. Thinking he'd be witty, Brice replied "Do you sell them by the seashore?"

Luckily, Gabrielle, a fellow Brady Bunch fan, got the joke. "No, smarty pants, I ship them out from my home to places all over the world. I don't think they'd sell so easily by the seashore. Why would people who are on the seashore need to pay for shells?"

"Good point," Brice admitted. "Where did you get that cute accent?"

Realizing that this guy was now flirting, Gabrielle became coy. "Ya like it? I'm a Tennessee girl."

The two began walking down the beach, finding out about each other.

The next morning, they met for omelets and coffee at a beach café. They continued meeting on the beach every morning, even though the early rising was making Brice a very exhausted boy.

They got to know each other, their hopes and dreams, their likes and dislikes. Whenever Brice had a night off from the restaurant, they enjoyed cooking dinner together at his place. Brice introduced Gabrielle to fancy dishes, artfully presented, and drizzled in exotic sauces. Gabrielle introduced Brice to staples from her childhood: soup beans, cornbread, tomato sandwiches, grits, sweet tea and all sorts of fried goodies.

One night, after Gabrielle had talked to her parents and was feeling particularly homesick, Brice surprised her with a dinner that could only be described as "country fusion." He combined the ingredients and techniques they both savored and made it into the best dinner Gabrielle had ever eaten. The spread included fried green tomatoes, breaded in sour dough bread crumbs and fresh herbs, grilled catfish on a bed of collard greens, sweet corn and pimento pudding and fried hush puppies with orange and honey butter. To wash it down, Brice made iced tea and sweetened it with a mango and lemon syrup. For dessert, he made banana pudding, using vanilla shortbread cookies and custard rather than the traditional vanilla wafers and instant pudding.

"Hick meets chic," is how the style was later described by a Florida food critic. Others tried to sum up the food as well as the owners' relationship. "Where the Appalachian Mountains meet the Florida Gulf" and "Heavenly Pairings" were just a couple of highlights from glowing reviews of the restaurant. It just worked! Gabrielle and Brice's relationship, the food, the atmosphere, it was perfect!

Six months after their initial meeting, the two decided to become business partners. It was tough going at first. They remained in their jobs until the restaurant's grand opening. All their free time was put into restoring the building for The Old Dock, obtaining appropriate permits and licensing and developing a unique menu.

All the hard work paid off. One year after their initial meeting, the two were running a successful restaurant and planning their wedding. Marlene's parents ate at the restaurant at least twice a week and were treated like royalty. They even had a favorite table overlooking the water. Whenever they were on their way to the restaurant, Marlene's mom would let Gabrielle or Brice know they were coming and the table was always ready by the time they arrived. Luckily, Mark told the hostess that they were dining with Marlene's parents and was able to secure the favorite table.

Soon after they were seated, a waitress brought a pitcher of ice water, four glasses of iced tea, and a crab dip appetizer. Mark took the liberty of ordering something to start off their meal. The crab dip was amazing. It was served in a crock and came with toasted bread rounds. It was creamy and cheesy and filled with sweet lump crab meat. As Marlene munched on crab dip atop crunchy bread, she couldn't help but notice that her parents and Mark kept exchanging knowing glances between each other. It was a little annoying, like there was some joke among the Florida people that she couldn't be in on. She knew something was up!

Marlene ordered her favorite meal of all times: grilled shrimp, stuffed with crab and bread crumbs, and wrapped in bacon, Nappa Cabbage coleslaw, and hush puppies slathered in honey-butter. Everybody else at the table ordered fish entrees. They were all enjoying their meal and the conversation, but there was an obvious nervous tension in the air. The tension grew as the meal progressed. Marlene was totally in the dark about what was happening, but she knew that it was something major!

After their meal, the waitress brought dessert menus to Marlene's parents. Marlene always got the blackberry trifle with muscadine wine custard and a cappuccino, so she didn't need to see a dessert menu, but it was strange that the waitress didn't give one to her or Mark.

Ever since she could remember, Marlene's parents had shared desserts. It was so cute to watch them. They'd peruse the menu to find something that they both found tempting, and then order one dessert and two forks. Together they'd huddle close as they savored every bite. When there was nothing but that last little morsel left, they spend about five minutes urging each other to take it. Usually her mom got it!

As her parents discussed the merits of peanut butter pie versus bread pudding with caramel sauce, their waitress brought a carry out box and a drink carrier with two cups of coffee in it. Mark had gotten two blackberry trifles and cappuccinos to go. Now Marlene was really curious about what was going on. Marlene's dad said, "See you two later," and gave Mark a big wink. Mark quickly paid the bill. They said goodbye to her parents, and they were out the door.

Suddenly, Mark seemed very nervous. He was usually so calm and methodical. This was really out of sorts for him! He grabbed a canvas tote from his car and the two embarked down the beach. There was a soft breeze making the palm trees sway, and the waves gently caressed the sand. Often the beach was filled with the sound of crashing surf, but that night it was as if the sea were being so respectful of them as to not disturb their moment.

Hand-in-hand, the two found a secluded spot away from the din of all the hotels and restaurants. Mark pulled a picnic blanket from the canvas bag and spread it on the sand. The pair sat close to savor their dessert and coffee. It was over dessert and coffee that they professed their love for the very first time. Mark admitted that he'd been certain of his feelings for a while, but wanted to wait until the perfect moment to tell her.

After they finished their dessert and cappuccino, Mark told Marlene that he had something else that he must tell her. "I'm not sure what you're reaction is going to be" Mark nervously confessed.

"Oh no, he's married! He's gay! He loves me, but doesn't see a future for us!" Marlene was now more nervous than Mark as she thought of every bad ending that their romance could have.

Mark took a deep breath, then began. "I think that one of us is going to have to move in order for this thing to work. It should be easier for me to move my real estate business than for you to open a shop somewhere else. There's a big boom in mountain real estate. I want to move my business to Coleman; and there's one more thing."

Mark reached into his coat pocket. When his hand emerged, it was trembling and holding a small box. "Marlene Prescott, will you be my wife?"

Chapter 23

After speaking more with the adoption agency, Tom and Dorothy were confident that they'd be getting their baby. They'd gone through all the red tape. Tom and Dorothy were told that they should be able to go to Tennessee to get the baby within the next two weeks. In the meantime, the agency had e-mailed pictures of her.

The parents-to-be were enamored with her pictures! She was so beautiful! Her name was Darla. The agency said they could change her name, but Tom and Dorothy decided to keep her first name. She was not given a middle name by her mother. They planned to use Breanne for a middle name. Of course, she'd take their last name when the adoption became official.

Despite not having the greatest prenatal care, Darla was a full term baby and in excellent health. She had deep blue eyes and a perfect little round bald head. Her lips were full and pink like a rosebud. Tom and Dorothy couldn't wait to get their hands on her! They had spent hours gazing longingly at her picture. Tom and Dorothy knew that she was already theirs. She was the little girl whom God wanted them to have! They already felt a connection to her that only parents and a child could share.

The first time they thought they'd be getting a baby, Tom and Dorothy bought a whole room of nursery furniture. In an act of faith they left it set up with the belief that the adoption agency would match them with a child. For the next couple of weeks they'd be busy getting diapers, bottles, blankets, and clothes. The nursery walls were bare white. Tom bought a few gallons of semi-gloss paint in the color of pink ballet slippers to make the room perfect for their little baby girl!

Dorothy's parents were coming in to help them get ready for Darla's homecoming. Her Mom and Dad still had a home in Coleman, but were almost never around. Since her Dad retired, they'd bought an RV and spent most of their time traveling. Their goal was to see every state in the union and every national park. Dorothy had a nice collection of postcards from various sights they'd seen. She was sure having a granddaughter would keep them put a little more, at least for her first few years of life. Her dad was already talking about trips they'd take with Darla when she got older.

Dorothy's brother and his wife would come up the week after they got Darla. Greg was ten years younger than Dorothy and had just gotten married the year before. He married a girl from Birmingham, Alabama; and they lived down there. His wife was anxious to start a family and hoped that being around Darla would give Greg the baby aches.

Dorothy decided to go ahead and tell Larry that she planned to take a few weeks off after the adoption. Since she wanted the whole world to know her good news, she told him in front of Patsy. Larry seemed genuinely thrilled for Dorothy and agreed to six weeks of adoption leave with three more weeks of working part time. Patsy congratulated Dorothy, and then headed to the phone.

Dorothy tried to call Marlene with the good news. Marlene didn't answer her cell phone, so Dorothy called Marlene's parents' house. With it being her last night, Dorothy figured she might be packing. Her mother told Dorothy that Marlene was out with Mark and might have a big announcement to make when she got home.

Meanwhile, Patsy set The Hens phone chain in motion. "Dorothy is going to be getting a baby soon. Don't you bet that Marlene is going to stay down in Florida to have her baby? Then she'll bring it back to Coleman to be raised by Dorothy."

Chapter 24

Marlene's flight was scheduled for seven in the morning. She should have tried to get a little sleep, but her mind was racing. For the past several years, her life had been very predictable. When ones existence revolved around her work, rather than another person, things were quite controllable. Was Marlene ready to get a little zany and switch things up?

She gazed at the glimmering jewel on her left hand, thought about the heartfelt words that passed between them, and knew that it was time! Love no longer seemed scary. It felt safe and comfortable. In a moment, Marlene decided that marriage wasn't a gamble. She and Mark's love and commitment were a sure thing. Marlene was ready to be with this man forever!

So far, only Marlene and Mark's parents knew about their engagement. Marlene came home in the wee hours of the morning to find her mom and dad waiting up for her at the kitchen table. They knew of Mark's plans and had hoped with all their hearts she'd accept his proposal. They knew that their daughter was completely capable of taking care of herself, but liked the idea that she'd have someone after they passed on.

Mark's parents lived in Cincinnati. Last summer Marlene and Mark stayed at their house for a few days. The four of them had a wonderful time visiting Cincinnati landmarks, going to a Reds' game, and spending a day riding roller coasters at King's

Island. They loved Marlene and couldn't have been more thrilled about the engagement.

Mark came to the house that morning where they all had breakfast. As they ate their French toast and scrambled eggs, Mark sprang another surprise on them. He revealed that he was the mysterious gentleman who had purchased the building beside of Marlene's pie shop! Marlene had told him about wanting the building once on the phone. Using a chain of connections he'd made in the business, he was able to make the transaction without anyone in Coleman knowing about it. He planned to use the upstairs as a real estate office and Marlene could expand her shop in the downstairs. "What would you have done if Marlene had said no?" Marlene's father asked.

"Hey, real estate's almost never a bad investment. I guess I could have sold it to Marlene. If she wouldn't have accepted my proposal, at least she might have bought some property from me."

Marlene's dad slapped Mark on the back. "Spoken like a true real estate mogul."

"Or," Mark added, "I might have moved to Coleman, put a business in beside of Marlene and stalked her till she fell in love with me."

After breakfast, the four of them rode to the airport. Mark would be flying to Coleman soon to begin the remodeling process on the future home of his and Marlene's new businesses. Last night, they decided that their wedding would be in six months, on the beach, right at the spot where they had their nighttime proposal picnic.

Chapter 25

Thanks to a layover in Atlanta, Marlene had a little time to kill. She bought a wedding magazine from a news stand and thumbed through it to get ideas for her upcoming nuptials. It was so funny that her thoughts were so focused on her business and its future growth when she embarked on her trip. A few days later, making her return flight, she was browsing through a bridal magazine like a twenty-something. Later she told Dorothy and Allison, "I bet people in the airport thought I was planning a wedding for my daughter!"

Marlene thought of herself as a "mature bride."

After studying the magazine and folding down pages she wanted to visit again, Marlene's thoughts did turn to her business. Months after adjusting to the fact that she probably would not be getting the building next door, she actually had the building next door! As sweet as Mark's proposal was, his buying the building just sort of put a bow on it all. He went above and beyond to prove that he actually listened when Marlene talked about her dreams for the future. It was such a risky and unselfish thing to do, and the symbolism of it was not lost on Marlene. She knew that Mark was willing to risk it all for their future together and put himself on the line, personally, professionally, and financially.

Marlene got home late in the afternoon. She went by Cutie Pies to make sure everything was okay. Charity zeroed in on her diamond the minute she walked through the door. Marlene was dying to dish the details with her, but decided she wanted to do it when all the girls could be together.

Charity was gung-ho for having dinner that night. Marlene called Allison and Dorothy, who were both free also. She told Dorothy she had big news, and Dorothy told Marlene that she had bigger news. They decided to have pizza at Marlene's house. That way they could laugh and talk as loud and as much as they wanted.

They all met at Marlene's house at six. She had the neatest house, perfect for a successful single gal. It was a Mediterranean style home. The outside was beige stucco and stone with an orange terra cotta tile roof. To enter her home you passed through an iron gate which led to a small courtyard filled with all sorts of plants and a koi fish pond. From the pond sprung a gushing fountain. A cement bench where Marlene could relax and enjoy the peaceful sounds of the waterfall sat beside the koi pond. The stone walkway ran through the middle of the courtyard and led to a beautiful hand-carved door. Inside, it was an open floor plan. The ceilings were high, and the walls were painted in bright sunny hues. Her friends always felt like they were on vacation when they visited Marlene's house. It looked like something that should be sitting on a sunny beach off the coast of Italy or Greece.

Marlene had pizzas in the oven and had also made a huge salad in a wooden bowl. For dessert, she'd brought an orange cream pie from the shop. They sat in the floor on big pillows and munched on salad while waiting for the pizzas to bake. Marlene excused herself only to return flashing a huge rock on her hand! The girls all screamed like a bunch of teenagers and congratulated her. Then, of course, they had to know the details.

She told them of their walk on the beach and the proposal. Mark had also stowed away a little bottle of champagne and two glasses in that canvas bag. Marlene said it was like a movie. They kissed and held each other and sipped champagne as they watched the sun rise over the ocean and planned their future.

After the girls gushed over Marlene's engagement, Dorothy announced her good news. She had been so emotional ever since she found out she and Tom were getting a daughter. Dorothy was a basket case when she told the girls whom she'd grown to love like sisters. By the time she was through, they were all crying, especially Charity, whose hormones were in overdrive.

For the rest of the night, they ate pizza, looked at things Marlene had picked from the wedding magazine, and planned baby showers for Dorothy and Charity. Allison jokingly said, "Gee, I feel a little left out here. I don't have any exciting event coming up!"

Little did Allison know that she'd be having a big birthday bash in just over two weeks.

"Oh, I can't believe I forgot to tell you all this!" Marlene jumped in. "Mark bought the building next door to me."

Charity noted, "Well, I don't know this guy, but he must be something else if he can purchase a business in this town and none of The Hens know about it!"

"Speaking of The Hens," Dorothy said, "You girls won't believe what they've been saying about Marlene!"

"I can only imagine," Marlene quipped.

Dorothy looked at Marlene, so happy and carefree. At what seemed like a time when their lives were perfect, she hated to even bring up the topic, but she had to. What Dorothy was about to reveal could only put a damper on their jovial mood, but Marlene needed to know.

"Pregnant, they're saying I'm pregnant?" Marlene, who usually let anything The Hens said bounce right off, was hot and bothered over this one! Dorothy told her about all the supposed facts they'd put together. Allison wasn't at all amused by the rumor that Gary was the father.

At first, Allison was all for getting some Hens on a conference call and setting them straight. Then she got all militant. "We ought to march right over to Millie's right now. Their canasta club is meeting at her house tonight. We'll line them up firing squad style and give every one of them a tongue lashing like they've never heard."

Allison had them all pretty fired up until Marlene convinced everyone that it might be better to do nothing; as in let The Hens keep at it until they pooped in their own nests, so to speak! A twinkle in Marlene's eye told them that she was up to something. It was gonna be subtle, but it was going to be good!

Chapter 26

Marlene had so much to do in the next few months: Allison's birthday party, baby showers, renovation of the building next door, and of course, her wedding. First order of business was to find another employee.

Charity would be taking a nine week maternity leave which would begin sometime around the date of Marlene's wedding. It would take a big weight off Marlene's shoulders if she could hire and train her new person as soon as possible.

Charity had set the bar pretty high. Marlene needed to find somebody just as capable and efficient. This person would have numerous responsibilities. One of the most important tasks would be to do Marlene's nautical wedding pie display. Marlene wanted to relax and enjoy her wedding. That would not include having to cater her own wedding. Whoever she hired would be asked to travel to Florida and do a display that Marlene had dreamed up in her head.

Marlene envisioned pies of various sizes in flavors of tropical fruits, covered with fluffy meringue. Some would be sprinkled with toasted coconut, others dusted in colored sugars. Still more would be topped with twists of crystallized ginger or candied fruit peels. The large center pie would be adorned with fresh flowers. It would be a sight fit for pie heaven! As she described her elaborate pie dreams Marlene claimed, "My goal is to make wedding cake seem passé and obsolete."

Taking a recommendation from Charity, Marlene set up an interview with one of Charity's classmates from the technical institute. He was a gentleman named Adam who attended culinary classes in hopes of finding a second career. After retiring from a career in the automotive industry in Detroit, Adam and his wife came to Coleman to retire in the mountains where they grew up.

It didn't take long for Marlene to take a liking to Adam. He told her that he had always loved to cook. In his Detroit suburb he was known as "The Virginia Pie Guy" because of his accent, and he was always taking pies around to his neighbors. He brought a pie for Marlene to sample. It was his special cherry chocolate cordial pie. The crust was made from butter and chocolate cookie crumbs. The filling was composed of tart fresh cherries swimming in sweet syrup. Adam got the idea when he and his wife were in Michigan, where cherries were plentiful. A slice of the pie was like eating a box of chocolate covered cherries!

Marlene sure wanted to hire Adam. If he were agreeable to catering her wedding, it was a done deal. "Adam, I have one final question. As I mentioned, one of the reasons I'm hiring a new employee is that I am getting married in six months. It just wouldn't seem right for me to serve anything other than pies for my own wedding. Would you be willing to do the pies for my wedding if I pay travel expenses? I'll even pay for your wife to come with you."

Adam was not only willing, but eager to do Marlene's wedding pies. She told him about her plans to break into the special occasion pie market, and he thought it was a brilliant idea. He also saw the trip to Florida as a huge perk. "Wait till my wife hears that we're going to Florida. She'll be so excited!"

Adam filled out all the necessary forms, and they set up a training schedule. With that matter taken care of, it was on to the next order of business.

With Allison's birthday quickly approaching, Gary and Marlene had to get everything finalized. He'd found some pie pans and display pieces, which he delivered to Cutie Pies. Allison had told him about the big talk that he'd been carousing around town making babies. When Gary showed up to deliver the pans, Charity was at the front counter. "Here to see your girlfriend?" she asked while winking at Gary.

"No, this visit isn't conjugal, just business."

Marlene played up the situation when she walked in. "Hey handsome, aren't we getting a little brave with these midday trysts? Why there's probably some Hen spying on us at this very moment."

Gary responded, "Dare we go back in the kitchen to look at these new pans and display plates?"

Charity went back with them. "I'm not suspicious of you two, I promise. I just want to see what Gary brought."

Charity and Marlene were thrilled with the pieces that he found. "These are fantastic!" they both declared.

"Good," said Gary. "They should be perfect for Allison's party."

A customer entered, so Charity returned to the counter while Marlene and Gary discussed more details about Allison's birthday surprise. The customer was none other than Leila's sister, Lorna. One thing that could be said about The Hens, they may have talked trash about Marlene; but they still bought her pies. Lorna ordered six pies for Leila and her husband Bill's anniversary party. She ordered a lemon meringue, chocolate French silk, coconut cream, Dutch apple, blueberry crumble and peach tart. As Charity was jotting down the order, Marlene and Gary came out from the kitchen. Seeing Lorna made them both chuckle. This would surely become the scoop of the day for The Hens.

Lorna, being the curious lady she was, inquired about Marlene's new ring. "It's just a little something I got on a trip to Florida last week," Marlene told her while smiling from ear to ear.

Lorna got in her car and called her sister. "Leila, Gary and she came out of the back together, and they were laughing! Oh, and Marlene has this huge diamond on her left ring finger. She says she got it in Florida. I bet you a hundred dollars it's from that no good Gary. Can you believe him, running around on his wife with her best friend? You know Allison doesn't have her ring anymore. I bet he sold it to get Marlene that big old thing she's wearing! He and Marlene came out of the back together when I was ordering pies. I hate to think what they were doing back there; but it sure didn't look good, their coming out laughing. If you ask me, they looked a little disheveled."

For the next few days, a steady flock of Hens streamed in and out of Cutie Pies. An interest in eyeing Marlene's ring set off an insatiable craving for pie. Marlene really didn't mind. It was great for business. Every time one of them came in, Marlene gave them exactly what they wanted. Being left-handed, Marlene had an aptitude for shoving that rock in their faces as she handed them change. They all got a big eyeful of that ring so they could gander, appraise, and speculate.

Jan allowed that it was just plain gaudy. Patsy thought it was fake. Millie liked the diamonds, but not the way they were set in the prongs. How many carats was it? Most Hens thought the center solitaire was about two and a half carats. The baguettes looked to be nearly a half carat each.

"Probably at least a twenty thousand dollar ring," according to Lorna.

"Not if it's rhinestones," added Patsy.

There was a near consensus that the ring was from Gary. Leila guessed otherwise. She thought Marlene bought if for herself in Florida. "It's to help protect her honor when she begins to show. She's probably bought herself a wedding band, too. That way, she can go off to Florida again, come back wearing that band, and say she got married down there. Supposedly this man works down there. That's why nobody in Coleman has ever seen him. There's no such man! We'll never see him!"

Chapter 27

Tom and Dorothy were proud new parents! Really, proud didn't even begin to describe it! They were gushing, blubbering, whipped, and enamored. This baby girl had them both plumb tickled!

Yesterday, they drove to Tennessee and picked her up! There will never be another moment in their lives as great as when that sweet angelic little baby was placed in their arms! Darla was a plump four month old with a curiosity about her world and a repertoire of adorable facial expressions and cute baby sounds.

On the drive home from Tennessee, Dorothy rode in the back seat with her while Tom drove. All the way home, they sang lullabies and told Darla about her new mommy and daddy. There was never an awkward moment. The bond was immediate and permanent. This was their little girl! Of all the little girls and parents in the world, God put Darla and them together; and it was a match made in heaven!

Both Dorothy's and Tom's parents stayed at their house the first night to get acquainted with their new grandbaby. After that, Tom and Dorothy were going to try the parenting thing on their own. Except for doing some photographs at Allison's party, Tom was taking the rest of the week off.

Tom and Dorothy couldn't wait to take Darla to the party and show her off. So far, she had the best temperament. They wondered if she were just testing her new parents and maybe in a few days would start getting fussy. Whatever happened, she was all theirs, and they loved her! For the past twenty-four hours, she'd been passed from one set of adoring arms to another.

Tom had never looked so handsome to Dorothy as when he held his baby girl and looked into her perfect little face. There was softness about him Dorothy had never seen before. Not only had they fallen in love with Darla, their love and respect for each other had deepened. Is there anything more attractive than a man doting on his child? Dorothy didn't think so! She was sure their relationship would be tested with the challenges of parenthood, but she knew they could do it!

The next week, Allison and Marlene were throwing a baby shower for Dorothy at the church. It was so wonderful for Dorothy to share Darla with friends who had been with her through the ups and downs of infertility and adoption. Dorothy couldn't decide between the two of them, so little Darla had two Godmothers to spoil her rotten!

Chapter 28

Perry Coleman was the man for whom Coleman was named. He was probably the richest man to ever live in those parts. His story was an illustration of the American Dream. Perry was Scottish and his wife, Ruth, was American. As the story goes, Perry and his wife met when she and her family were touring the British Isles. Ruth's father owned many of the coal mines in this area and had made a fortune. On the other hand, Perry's father was a poor fisherman. Perry assumed he'd follow in his footsteps.

Most aristocratic families would not approve of such a union. Perry seemed to have so little to offer, but Ruth's father saw something he liked in Perry Coleman. First of all, anyone could see that he loved Ruth with all his heart and would do anything to make her happy. Perry also had pride and ambition. Ruth's father saw a spark in Perry's eyes and sensed a fire in the young man's belly. This young man had spirit and would make something of himself if given the chance.

Ruth's father helped Perry attain a student visa to attend college in the United States. He financed Perry's education with one stipulation. Perry had to work for him for at least five years. Being good with numbers, Perry received his degree in accounting from Marshall University. Perry's philosophy was to be as scrupulous with Ruth's father's money as he had been with his own. He also felt strongly that employees who were treated well would be happy and productive.

Perry combed the company ledgers with scrutiny and precision. If there were a place where money was not being wisely spent, he found it. In the first year alone, Perry saved Ruth's father enough to acquire another mine. They became the most efficiently run mining operation in the country. Their mines were safe; the wages were excellent; and the miners were allowed to have a say before there was ever such thing as a miner's union.

Perry eventually became a partner in the business and later took it over. His mines served as the gold standard for the rest of the country. Men moved from other parts of the United States and even other countries to have the good fortune of working for Perry Coleman.

Perry and Ruth built a stately home on a hillside that could be seen from Main Street. In their will, they left their mansion to the town of Coleman. The home's main floor had been divided into two large banquet halls. Gary booked the Black Diamond Room for Allison's party.

When Lorna picked up the pies for Leila's anniversary gathering, she told Charity that their party was going to be in the White Birch Ballroom. So, The Hens would be sharing the Coleman Mansion with Allison's guests. It would prove to be a very interesting evening! There was fear that the mansion might not be big enough to house both groups peacefully without a cat fight or Hen pecking!

Darla's outfit for the party was befitting of a wonderful baby girl who was about to be introduced to the people of her hometown. Tom and Dorothy went to Langrid and bought it the night after they found out they'd be getting her. It was a forest green and cream dress with a little matching sweater to go over it. The accessories were the best part. Darla was wearing a forest green and cream plaid beret, cream sweater tights and tiny cloth shoes that matched her beret. Darla grinned at her parents as they oohed and ahhed over her outfit. Her cheeks were all pink and fat, and her eyes were sparkling like two brilliant sapphires. Darla seemed to already know that she was something special!

Chapter 29

Mark flew in to begin work on the building he'd purchased. He decided to split his time between Florida and Virginia until the wedding. That would give him an opportunity to spend more time with Marlene, renovate the building, and begin establishing contacts in Coleman. The building had a working bathroom, kitchen, and heating system. So, when Mark was in Coleman, he planned to live there.

He was at the Coleman Mansion helping Marlene set up the most grand pie display that the town has ever seen. The pie plates were beautiful glazed pottery in muted blues, reds, greens and yellows. Several pie plates were placed in a circular pattern on the table. In the middle was the large pie. Others were on a display piece that sort of looked like a large antique lazy Susan. All together Marlene had made over a dozen varieties of pies for Allison's birthday. Hopefully, others in attendance would see what she'd done and maybe book her for big events. Just in case, there was a basket of business cards on the table.

Marlene gave Charity the day off because her husband had gotten home the night before. They were coming to the party later. It was finally okay to tell everyone that Charity was expecting. It was a good thing! She was starting to show!

After Marlene and Mark had set up the pies, she went to a restroom to change into her outfit for the party. She came out looking gorgeous in a pair of black pants, black patent leather high heeled boots and a gray angora sweater with silver threads running through it. She arranged her hair in an elegant French twist with loose tendrils in the front. Mark looked equally handsome in an off white cashmere sweater and fine gauge corduroy trousers finished off by a pair of meticulously polished crocodile loafers.

Originally, the party was supposed to be a surprise; but the surprise was spoiled a couple of days before when Allison took the call confirming their reservation of the banquet room. "You must be Mark," Allison and Gary said almost in unison. As they shook hands and got acquainted, the deejay came in to set up.

Marlene helped Allison compose a play list for the deejay. They decided that disco music might set the tone for some good times. They got amused when they imagined some of the party guests "getting down" to the songs they'd picked. The deejay suggested a limbo contest. It was his experience that it always got guests in a festive mood and got people up out of their seats. Most of the crowd was not going to be going very low, except for Nita Oliver, who taught yoga. Still, it would be good entertainment as long as nobody pulled or broke anything. Dr. Tate, the only chiropractor in Coleman, would be there. He should have brought his appointment book to schedule Monday morning adjustments and alignments for partiers who had gone lower than they should have in the limbo contest.

After everything was squared away with the deejay, Allison and Gary went to the lobby to greet party-goers as they came in. Guests for Allison's party and "The Hen" party trickled in together. Thanks to some pre-party preening at Leila's, The Hens were all donning their signature festive look. The hair was teased as high as an elephant's eye. All of them had the same hairstyle, just in different colors. For extra pizzazz, they used gold glitter hairspray. The sheer volume of hair product used may have posed a danger. "There's a hole in the ozone over

Coleman now!" noted Gary. "Let's just pray nobody lights a match in here."

If possible, the makeup was worse than the hair. The Hens were all spackled and painted with colors that befitted a circus tent and not a face. The signature blue eye shadow was applied with a heavy hand. Their cheeks were a bright fuchsia flush. The lips were all so shiny and crimson red that it looked as though each of them had two pieces of bloody beef liver hanging from their mouths. Last week, Big-Lots in Langrid had a close-out on some pink press-on nails. Their fingertips all bore press-on nails the length of talons and the color of bubble-gum.

Patsy did her nails Friday morning to give them a test run before the big party. For the rest of the day, Patsy was impaired by the long candy-colored claws. Dorothy had to open her mail, pop the top on her soft drink and scratch her nose. Dorothy sure hoped those things fell off before Monday.

It appeared they all agreed to ditch the shapeless clothing along with the girdles. They went a little tighter, a little shorter and flesh was jiggling all over the place. Most were stuffed so tight into their outfits that there was no room for expansion. If one of them popped a button, it would have come off with the force of a bullet fired from a pistol. Somebody could lose an eye! Before the party, everyone thought The Hens wore big tent dresses because they had no fashion sense. Now, everyone knew. It was a service to mankind. It was for the greater good. Nobody needed to see what they'd been hiding under those big dresses!

There was mass confusion when Hens saw Allison and Gary together with Allison wearing a new and improved wedding ring. They quickly got to work concocting a fresh set of rumors. Like a news crew, they put together information as it came in and tried to stay abreast of what was going on.

Bobby's Café catered both events. Missy Bergner was setting up the food in the White Birch Ballroom for The Hens. Missy Bergner was sort of a Hen wannabe. She was not quite as devious as a Hen, which prevented her from actually starting rumors. Missy was not above perpetuating a rumor once it was started, but fear kept her from stating anything as factual. She used lots of words like "allegedly" and "supposedly" to qualify her statements. Her lingo was like that of a political candidate trying to appease both sides. Missy sort of sat on the fence that divided "The Hen" and non-Hen world. She was "the noncommittal Hen."

Nola Hoffman was setting up food for Allison's party. She and Missy crossed paths in the hallway where Missy filled her in on the latest. "Now I don't know if this is true. I'm just talking after Lorna, but apparently there was something going on between Gary and Marlene. Evidently, Allison and Gary split up for a while. It seems they're back together because they were standing in the entrance beside each other tonight. Leila claims that Allison didn't wear her ring for a few weeks; and all of the sudden, Marlene had this huge diamond. Well, tonight, Allison's got this big rock on that looks like the one Marlene was wearing last week!"

An urgent diaper change kept Dorothy and Tom from arriving to the party on time. They wound up walking in with Patsy and Larry. When they entered, Allison and Gary made a bee line to Tom and Dorothy so that they could see Darla. She performed perfectly for them, cooing and grinning. Patsy seemed stunned to see Allison and Gary standing together. She wished Allison a happy birthday. In an unexpected move, Allison told Patsy that everyone from their party was welcome to come by her birthday party. "You guys have to see what Marlene's done!" Allison told her.

Allison set out the bait. They just had to wait and see if The Hens would take it.

Chapter 30

Whoever said "curiosity killed the cat" never met a Hen. As predicted, a bunch of Hens came by to see what was going on in the Black Diamond Room. The Hens themed their menu around foods on toothpicks. They entered Allison's party with plates full of meatballs on toothpicks, olives on picks, pickles on picks, cheese cubes on picks, and speared fruit. The plates they carried resemble little porcupines. In an ironic twist, they entered to find Marlene holding Darla. With no effort to cover their sneaky intentions, The Hens began openly whispering to each other.

Gary, who was petrified to address a crowd, elected Marlene to give the welcome speech. Allison urged her to take whatever liberties she wanted to make the speech memorable and gratifying. The deejay stopped the music and handed the microphone to Marlene. As Marlene stared into the beady little eyes of The Hens, she realized what a golden opportunity it was.

"Hello everyone, because Gary hates to give speeches and I, on the other hand, love to talk, I'll be doing the honors of thanking everyone here for coming out tonight. We're all here to celebrate Allison's birthday. She's given so much of herself as a wife, a mother, a member of her church and community, and as a friend. Allison is an amazing woman who truly deserves to be celebrated. Allison has asked that I mention a few other celebrations going on in this room tonight. First of all, you may be wondering about the beautiful baby girl being passed around. Contrary to a widespread belief, I am not nor ever have been with child. Though I would certainly be proud to claim her, she belongs to Dorothy and Tom. Her name is Darla. Dorothy and Tom finalized her adoption this week and are now blessed to be her proud and loving parents. You guys may have noticed a new face at Cutie Pies. She's my lovely and super talented co-worker, Charity, who's made herself invaluable to me. She's here tonight with her husband, Joe; and I'm happy to announce that the two of them are expecting. While I'm up here, I have a secret to confess. You all may have not been able to help but notice the devilishly handsome man I've been seen with tonight. We've been dating on the sly for years. We met in Florida and have had a long distance relationship. Mark asked me to marry him on my last trip to Florida, and I happily accepted! He is here tonight and will be moving to Coleman. Mark sells real estate; so if you're in the market, be sure to ask him for his card. Before I stop talking, I want to do a little shameless self-promotion. Hopefully, you've noticed the display of pies. Cutie Pies is now making special occasion pies. So, if you'd like such a display, please give me a call. Finally, I want to congratulate Leila and Bill, who are celebrating their anniversary in The White Birch Ballroom next door."

Marlene handed the microphone back to the deejay and breathed a sigh of relief. She managed to quickly and publicly clear up months of speculations without saying an unkind word to anyone. The Hens quietly slipped out of the room, red-faced and downtrodden. The pies were certainly a huge hit, but it seems that Marlene's sweetest offering was the huge slice of humble pie served up to The Hens! Is revenge a dish that is best served cold? Maybe not; Marlene served it up with warmth and wit and a satisfied Cheshire cat grin.

Chapter 31

Marlene and Mark had a beautiful seaside wedding. The wedding and reception ended a fun wedding weekend, full of festivities. Everything was planned perfectly down the last detail. The guest list was composed of family, very close friends from Coleman, people from Florida with whom Marlene and her parents had become friends, and Mark's close friends and business associates.

The celebrations began on Friday morning with a rehearsal brunch. The wedding party practiced the ceremony on the beach, and then had a quiche and mimosa brunch. One of Mark's friends offered his houseboat for the brunch. A buffet was lined up in the boat's kitchen, and tables were set up on top deck. There was crabmeat, spinach and three cheese quiches, fresh baked muffins, and a salad of honeydew, watermelon, and cantaloupe balls, mint leaves, and honey/lime dressing. After they ate, Mark's friend took them on a cruise down the intercoastal waterway.

The men stayed on the boat for an afternoon of fishing, hot wings and beer. The ladies had a spa party at the salon where Marlene's mom got her hair done. They had manicures, pedicures, and massages, while munching on finger sandwiches and sipping pomegranate martinis.

That night, everyone had a fabulous dinner. Being the geniuses they were at mixing cuisines, Gabrielle and Brice combined dishes from Marlene's region of the country with Cuban cuisine that was so much a part of Mark's heritage.

The dinner party was set up on the outside dining area of Gabrielle and Brice's restaurant. There were huge skillets of seafood paella, barbecued ribs, fried plantains, roasted sweet potatoes, red beans with yellow rice, fried chicken, cheese grits, corn muffins and a relish of corn, black beans and mangos.

Right in the spot where Mark had proposed, they exchanged their vows. Marlene had the preacher from her church fly down to perform the ceremony. In a light-hearted reference to finding love in their forties, they had the inside of each of their wedding bands inscribed with "Love is patient" from the Book of Corinthians.

Marlene outshone any young child bride. She looked gorgeous in a champagne colored cap sleeved gown with crystal beading. Her beach-tousled curls were held back from her face with a crystal encrusted headband. Mark wore a beige linen suit with a silk handkerchief tucked into the front pocket. Underneath his jacket was his signature crisp white shirt, casually unbuttoned at the top and no tie. Both the bride and groom walked down the sand in bare feet.

The Matrons of Honor: Allison and Dorothy; the Best Men: Mark's Dad and brother; and flower girl: Cicilly; and ring bearer: Garrett, also participated sans shoes. Thanks to the spa party, the girls had feet worthy of baring in public.

The groomsmen were dressed identically to Mark, except that their shirts were off-white. Allison and Dorothy wore lilac gowns with the same crystal beading as Marlene's dress, and both wore their hair up. Their hairstyles were in place with combs that had crystal beading. Again, the lady who did Marlene's momma's hair stepped in and gave them all picture perfect hairdos. This was not an easy feat, considering what the Florida humidity did to Dorothy's curls!

Cicilly and Garrett were adorable and perfectly behaved throughout the ceremony. Cicilly wore a plainer version of the bridesmaids' dresses and a rhinestone tiara. Instead of flower petals, she dropped shells from her basket. She knew she looked like a princess and was especially proud of her snazzy toenails. Gary brought Cicilly by the pedicure party just long enough to get a coat of lavender polish topped with purple glitter.

Garrett wore linen Bermuda shorts and a short sleeved white button up shirt. He looked extra sharp after he allowed the hairdresser to put a little gel on him. Gary said he even asked if he could wear some of his daddy's cologne. Little Darla was an absolute doll in a soft pink and yellow sundress that was hand-smocked and embroidered. She wore a white straw hat, trimmed in pink ribbon, and tiny yellow sunglasses. Dorothy's parents came down to Florida and helped watch her during all the festivities. She never got upset one time, except for when she was hungry or needed to be changed.

Gabrielle and Brice catered all the hors d'oeuvres. The food tables were under a tent. Gabrielle and Brice brought in an ice sculpture of two intertwined hearts for the center of the table. All up and down the table were little nibbles of seafood salads on bread rounds, medallions of beef, crab claws, country ham on buttered herb biscuits, peel-and-eat shrimp, pimento cheese on toast points and trays filled with fruits, vegetables and cheeses. The bartender from The Old Dock set up a tiki bar to mix frozen drinks and mojitos for adults and fruit smoothies for the kids. A small reggae band played beside the bar.

Charity's baby girl had arrived two weeks before. They took lots of pictures and video from the wedding to share with her. Adam proved to be worth his weight in gold! Marlene closed Cutie Pies for a week, which gave Adam several days in Florida to work on the pies. Gabrielle and Brice generously allowed Adam to use the kitchen at their house, which rivaled any restaurant cooking facility. Adam and Marlene spent many hours going over recipes and garnishes, and discussing the overall look she wanted.

In the end, Marlene just turned him loose and let him work his magic. In the days before the wedding, Marlene honored her promise not to interfere in the pies. She stayed away from Brice and Gabrielle's kitchen, putting her trust in Adam's abilities. Adam did not disappoint!

Guests oohed and ahhed as they entered the food tent and saw the extraordinary pie table. In the center, on a large pedestal, was a sugared grapefruit pie with candied citrus peels, slices of grapefruit coated in sugar and bright gerbera daisies on the top. Several other pies, all in luscious tropical flavors and topped by artfully arranged garnishes lined the table. Some were on pedestals, others on plates, and there was even a platter of mini tarts in various flavors. In a nod to both Mark and Marlene's grandparents, Adam made some guava empanadas dusted with cinnamon and sugar. The little fried pies filled with moist fruit were the Cuban version of the fried pies Marlene and her grandmother had first made in that old farmhouse kitchen.

The groom's pie was a chocolate and almond crust filled with chocolate and amaretto cream filling and topped with crushed almonds, sweetened almond flavored whipped cream and chocolate shavings. On the same table as the groom's pie was a basket of wedding favors. Each guest received a little gift box that included a golf ball inscribed with Mark and Marlene's names and the wedding date, a sand dollar and a tiny pecan tart wrapped in cellophane and tied with gossamer ribbon.

The best surprise of Mark and Marlene's wedding day was a gift from her parents. They had an artist friend build a sand replica of a bride and groom standing in front of a beautiful sand castle. The four foot tall creation stood outside of the reception tent.

The wedding was just like Marlene: fun, sentimental and elegant without being over-the-top. All the guests seemed to be in agreement that it was the most beautiful and unique wedding they'd ever attended. Everything was perfect. The service was lovely and meaningful; the flowers and food were too-die-for;

the weather was balmy and clear; and there wasn't a Hen in sight!

The dream wedding was followed by the trip of a lifetime. Mark and Marlene boarded a plane bound for Italy the next morning. For three weeks, they toured the country, basked on the beaches, hiked the mountains, toured the vineyards and savored the cuisine. Some truly wonderful pies came after their trip: tiramisu, cinnamon mocha cappuccino, cannoli, peach Bellini and layered spumoni.

Their honeymoon proved to be productive in many ways, or maybe it was more like reproductive. Although they came back with wonderful souvenirs for all their friends and family, the best honeymoon memento would come later . . . as in about nine months! Dorothy felt like the oldest new mom in town. Now, Marlene had her beat!

The Hens didn't get much right, but for once they were totally on target. Those change of life babies can surprise you. In this case, it was a wonderful surprise! Marlene had a feeling that it was going to be a girl. Wouldn't it be funny if Darla, Charity's baby and Marlene's child became good friends? If they did, Coleman would never be the same!

Did The Hens stop practicing their evil ways after the party? Marlene's nonconfrontational ways didn't exactly stop them. Squelched may be a better way to describe it. They were not quite as potent and Marlene was no longer their number one target. Still, no one apologized to Marlene or admitted any wrongdoing. It was all okay with Marlene, Dorothy and Allison. They couldn't control what The Hens did. The only things over which they ever had power were their attitudes and reactions towards them. In the latest and hopefully final battle in Hens versus the three girlfriends, the girlfriends came out on top! The victory was sweet as pie!

Final Words from the Author

I cannot imagine having a better experience in getting my first book published. A huge "thank you" to Tammy Robinson Smith of Mountain Girl Press. Without you, my dream might never have come to fruition. Pam Keaton, your talent and imagination took Marlene from my mind's eye to the book's cover. Sally Crockett, your editing and proofreading truly helped make this book the best it could be.

I have to give an overdue thank you to Ruth Street, my wonderful high school English teacher. You made a big deal over my writing and I have never forgotten how special you made me feel!

Todd and Calli, I can never express just how much I love both of you. Todd, you are my soul mate. Calli, you have Mommy's heart forever! You two bring the greatest joy to my life! Mom and Dad, you both encouraged my creativity and pursuit of my passions. Mamaw, your tales of the mountains, mines, and days gone by make me proud of who we are. Above all, I am thankful to God for blessing my life so richly!

Finally, I want to thank my readers. I hope that your first trip to Coleman has been fun and memorable! You will have an opportunity to revisit Coleman and all of your favorite characters in the sequel on which I am currently working. Expect more twists, scandals, wacky incidents, and of course, another battle of Hens vs. The Friends!

Please check out my website at **http://lisahall-7.tripod.com**

Lisa Hall
Author

Take a second trip to Coleman, Virginia and
check up on Marlene and the girls in

Cheaters, Pies, and Lullabies

Nothing that anyone does in Coleman, Virginia goes without
notice. So, how long can cheating spouses commence to carrying on
without being caught? How does a new mother cope with evil stares
and nasty comments as her parenting skills come under attack?
Readers will find the answers to these and many other questions
in *Cheaters, Pies, and Lullabies*.

In this sequel to *Secrets, Lies, and Pies* readers revisit Coleman,
where they will be reunited with their favorite and not-so-favorite
characters. Some significant events have occurred in the lives of
Marlene, Dorothy, Allison, and Charity. While they weather winds
of change and storms of uncertainty, The Hens continue to meddle,
scrutinize and hypothesize.

The ladies are again pitted against The Hens, or at least most
of The Hens. In a dramatic chain of events, a few Hens flee the flock
to help Marlene, Dorothy, Allison and Charity catch a man who is
up to no good.

Motherhood, infidelity, and high tech spying, along with more
of Marlene's yummy pies and lots of The Hens' lies make this book
every bit as delicious as the first. If you loved *Secrets, Lies, and Pies*,
come back for a second slice!

Coming from Mountain Girl Press in 2008
Cheaters, Pies and Lullabies

To order more Mountain Girl Press titles
Go to **http://www.mountaingirlpress.com**

Emmybeth Speaks
Tammy Robinson Smith

Emmybeth Johnson is a nine year old girl who lives in Little Creek, Tennessee in the foothills of the Appalachian Mountains. Her story begins late in the summer of 1971. Emmybeth likes to know what is happening with the adults in her life and in the community in general.

She has a favorite "hidey hole" where she can listen as her mother, grandmother and the ladies from her church's sewing circle discuss the latest news and gossip from Little Creek. Emmybeth treats the reader to the "goings on" of the community from her naïve perspective, which is sometimes closer to the truth than she knows.

Emmybeth Speaks is a story about a community of women who band together to help a friend and her family in crisis. Emmybeth is a wonderful little witness and narrator for this phenomenon. It is her first brush with "Girl Power" and a lesson she won't ever forget.

Emmybeth loves her life in Little Creek and her family with all of her heart. She doesn't think her circumstances will ever change. When they do, the fallout confuses her but with the help of the women who surround her; she survives the change and endures. *Emmybeth Speaks* is a literary treat for all ages!

$10.95 U.S.
ISBN 978-0-9767793-0-8

The Zinnia Tales

Kori E. Frazier   Lisa Hall   Susan Noe Harmon
Susanna Holstein   Pam Keaton   Jennifer Mullins
Tricia Scott   Tammy Robinson Smith   Mary McMillan Terry
Donna Akers Warmuth   Rebecca Lee Williams
P.J. Wilson   Tammy Wilson

Filled with stories that celebrate what it means to be an "Appalachian woman," *The Zinnia Tales* strike a note with anyone who has ever called the mountains home, or just wishes she lived there. Heralded as "Heartfelt, wise, and insightful," by Deborah Smith, *New York Times* bestselling author of *A Place to Call Home*, this collection of fictional tales highlights the struggles and triumphs of strong and determined Appalachian women. You will delight in the warmth of these stories which demonstrate the richness of the place where these women live their lives, and tell their stories.

Stories about women, written by Appalachian women writers, this rich group of works truly exemplify the Mountain Girl Press mission statement: *Stories that celebrate the wit, humor and strength of Appalachian women.*

$12.95 U.S.
ISBN: 978-0-9767793-1-5

Look for
Self-Rising Flowers
another short story collection written by Appalachian women writers, coming in October 2007